Books by Jean Little

MINE FOR KEEPS
HOME FROM FAR
SPRING BEGINS IN MARCH
WHEN THE PIE WAS OPENED
TAKE WING

Take Wing

Take Wing

by Jean Little

Illustrated by
Jerry Lazare

Little, Brown and Company
Boston   Toronto

Poetry on page 154
from "The Year Without a
Santa Claus" by Phyllis McGinley.

Published simultaneously in Canada
by Little, Brown & Company (Canada) Limited

PRINTED IN THE UNITED STATES OF AMERICA

For Ellen
who introduced me to James

A Friendship Is a Fragile Thing

A friendship is a fragile thing
— Like the dust of bloom on a butterfly's wing.
Presuming on it is like trying
To keep a butterfly from flying.
You cup your hands, try not to clutch,
But it is crippled by your touch,
By all the self-involved demands
Implicit in your closing hands.
Though friendship may stay acquiescent,
It is no longer iridescent.
There is no way man can contrive
To catch its loveliness alive
And keep it in captivity.
To glow, love must have liberty.
Yes, friendship is a fragile thing
— Like the dust of bloom on a butterfly's wing.

Yet, deep in love, there also lies
The bravery of butterflies.
Butterflies go through nights of storm
Migrating to a land that's warm.
They drift in brilliant frailty,
Testaments to mortality,
And all the while, they own the strength
To mount the wind, and come at length
Home again, their loveliness
Enduring through the journey's stress.
A treasured friendship also can
Survive the blundering of man.
Although it is a fragile thing,
It has the courage to take wing,
Dare to ride the dark, and come
Bravely home.

JEAN LITTLE

Contents

Take Wing

1

In the Middle of the Night

James had wet the bed again.

When she heard him calling her name softly, while she was still mostly asleep, Laurel knew what was wrong. She kept her eyes shut and her back turned.

"Laurie . . . Laurie!" James insisted, his voice rising.

Now he was tugging at her shoulder. Laurel gave a great sigh and flopped over on her back. She opened her eyes a crack.

"What's the matter?" she asked.

She could see him. He was shivering in the November wind that swept through her open window.

"Please, Laurie . . ." he said.

He was waiting for understanding to light her face but the hope in his eyes dulled as he watched her. Her mouth was set in a stubborn, unyielding line. She was going to make him explain. His head lowered. He tried to speak but choked over the words and had to stop to clear his throat. The hoarse little sound smote Laurel. She pushed back her warm covers.

"Why didn't you go to Mama?" she asked as she rolled out of bed.

James knew the answer to that question.

"I didn't want Mama. I wanted you."

"Okay, okay," Laurel said grumpily, not fooling James a bit.

She picked up her glasses automatically from the bedside table and put them on. Then she hurried across the room and banged down the window.

"Brrrrr!" she shivered, trying not to think of the cozy nest of blankets she had just left.

James scurried ahead of her into his small room next door. As she stripped the wet sheets off his bed, she scolded him.

"You ought to be ashamed," she told him tartly. "You're seven years old, James Ross. Lindsay's only four and she hasn't wet the bed in years."

"I know," James said. He really sounded ashamed and sorry but Laurel was aware that she had given him the same lecture often before. She relented a little when she saw how miserable he looked.

"I guess you can't help it or you wouldn't do it," she said more kindly.

She left him then to dump the wet things into the bathtub and fetch a clean sheet from the linen cupboard. When she came back, he was struggling with his pajama bottoms.

He had one foot in properly but his other foot had caught and he could not disentangle himself. Laurel came to his rescue with fresh impatience.

"You're so helpless," she snapped, giving him a none too gentle shove. "Get out of my way now."

He stood by watching while she briskly shook out the dry sheet and tucked it neatly into place. He had long since given up trying to help her. She was so much too quick for him.

When the bed was ready, she sent him to the bathroom "just in case."

"Hustle," she ordered, noticing how cold he looked.

He scuttled away through her room and down the hall. She waited, hands on hips, toe tapping. Suddenly, she grinned at her important, impatient stance and relaxed.

"You'd think I was Mama," she said to herself.

Not that she needed to pretend to be Mama to manage James. Mama herself admitted that Laurel handled James better than anyone else.

Perhaps it was because they looked so much alike. They had the same thin faces with high cheekbones, the same faintly brown skin — Mrs. Birch, the housekeeper, called them "sallow" — the same straight, glossy black hair, the same brown eyes. They both wore glasses, too, although James's were thicker and rounder. Laurel called him "Owl" sometimes.

"James, hurry up."

She called softly because of Lindsay, asleep in the bedroom at the far end of the hall, but James heard. He banged the bathroom door behind him before he realized why she had lowered her voice. Then, belatedly, he began to tiptoe. Laurel listened. There was no sound from Lindsay. She sighed with relief and then smiled at her little brother as he inched silently across the floor.

"Don't be such a nut," she gave him a loving spank that sent him speeding to bed.

"Laurie, tell me a story," he pleaded, pulling the covers up to his chin and peering at her with bright eyes over the heap of bedclothes.

"Are you out of your mind?" Laurel stared at him. "It's the middle of the night!"

James cuddled down expectantly. He knew that Laurel's outraged tone meant nothing at all. She wrapped herself up in his quilt, perched on the foot of the bed and began.

Laurel, whose compositions for school were stilted and unnatural, was a born storyteller. Mama claimed she had inherited the gift from Aunt Jessica, Mama's older sister. Mama and Aunt Jessica had shared a room when they were little girls and Aunt Jessica had told a serial story with a new chapter every night. James loved any tale Laurel told but, best of all, he liked her variations on the old story of the "teeny tiny woman" who lived in a teeny tiny house, went for a teeny tiny walk, found a teeny tiny apple, took it home to her teeny tiny house and put it safely away in her teeny tiny cupboard — only to hear a mysterious teeny tiny voice, outside her window, demanding, "Give . . . me . . . my . . . APPLE!" Finally, in desperation, the teeny tiny woman would shout, "TAKE IT!" And the story was over.

Sometimes, when Laurel told it, the teeny tiny woman

was a princess. Sometimes she was an Eskimo. Sometimes she found a teeny tiny hot dog. Sometimes she brought home a teeny tiny golden pear. But never, ever, was the mysterious teeny tiny voice explained.

Tonight, she was a duchess.

"And the teeny tiny duchess," finished Laurel, "gathered up every scrap of her teeny tiny courage and taking a deep teeny tiny breath, she popped her teeny tiny head out from under her teeny tiny satin pillow and shouted in her LOUDEST teeny tiny voice, 'TAKE IT!' "

James giggled happily and Laurel smiled at him.

"You go to sleep now," she told him and, turning out his light on her way, she went back to her own room.

But the warm nest she had deserted for James had grown cold. Laurel curled up, hugging her knees.

It was queer how Lindsay was so unlike herself and James. They were both dark while Lindsay had silky fair hair that curled and wide blue eyes. She had a snub nose exactly like Mama's and round pink cheeks that dimpled deeply when she laughed. Lindsay was like Mama in so many ways. They both loved to sing and to recite. Lindsay actually liked showing off for company. Laurel made a face at the thought. She and James did their best to stay out of sight until visitors had said good-bye and departed. Mama was still trying to get Laurel over what she called her "shyness" but she no longer bothered with James.

James had fallen asleep. Through the connecting door, Laurel could hear him breathing, slowly, evenly.

Laurel still remembered the day he had moved into that room. Mama had come to her just after Lindsay was born.

James had been three then. He had not started talking yet and he had only been walking for six months.

"I'd like to move him into the little gable room that opens out of yours, Laurel," Mama had told her. "He's still such a baby he needs someone to look after him. And you're so good with him. Mrs. MacIntyre was telling me just yesterday how well you handle him. I shouldn't depend on you so much but Lindsay needs me and I seem to get tired so quickly these days."

Laurel had been proud to be needed then. Before long, though, she had begun to worry about James. The little boy next door talked a mile a minute and he was just two. She went to Mama with her questions. Mama had not seemed to want to listen.

"He's just a baby, Laurie. Lots of children are different. He'll grow up fast enough once he gets started," Mama said.

He did begin to talk soon afterward. Laurel's anxiety eased. She was terribly pleased when his first word was "Laurie," although he could not pronounce the *r* properly.

Suddenly, not for the first time, Laurel Ross found herself wide-awake worrying over James. Her covers had twisted into an uncomfortable tangle. She kicked at them, trying to free herself. All the time, the things she had heard her parents say about James were replaying, like a tape recording, inside her head.

"He's slow maturing, that's all," Mama had said when he had to repeat kindergarten. "Miss Farmshaw doesn't understand him."

"He's sensitive. He's only just five . . ." Mama had said

that too. "He's only two!" "He's barely three." "He's still six, just a baby really."

Daddy used to say, "James is a slow starter. Any day now, he'll whiz ahead and surprise all of you."

When James failed first grade, Daddy had said, "He'd be fine if you and Laurel didn't baby him all the time, Susan."

"I think he's lazy — and they're letting him get away with it at that school," Daddy had growled less than a week ago.

Laurel knew James better than anyone else in the world. She knew he was no longer a baby. She knew, too, that he was not lazy. But he was different.

For the hundredth time, she tried to persuade herself that she was wrong. He was just like other boys his age. He was taller than most of them. He looked as ordinary as a little boy could except for his glasses — and lots of children wore glasses. He liked to play games . . .

Her glib thoughts stumbled as she saw James coming in last in almost every race, James getting the rules muddled in Kick the Can, James counting for Hide and Seek: "fifty-seven . . . fifty-eight . . . fifty-nine . . . thirty . . ."

"Stop it!" she told her troubled self crossly. "Mama and Daddy say he's all right — so he's all right. Think about flying instead."

Laurel had started her dream of flying when she was eight. She was almost too old to do it now but she held onto it all the more tightly because she knew, inside herself, that soon she would let it go.

She fixed her covers, nestled her head into her pillow, slid halfway into sleep and took wing.

She was not shut in an airplane. She did not even need to flap like a bird. She just soared out through the open window into the starry night as simply and beautifully as Peter Pan. Darkness turned to day. Winter turned to summer. Laurel skimmed through sparkling sunshine, over strange mountains and fairy-tale valleys. Small, unknown people stared up at her. They pointed her out. They shouted excited greetings and waved. She laughed and swooped low over them. Then she rose as lightly as the wind, somersaulted in the heady blue and came to rest on a cloud. Despite what she had learned about clouds at school, Laurel had discovered that, when she was flying, they held her weight easily and were as soft and bouncy as feather-beds.

Her flight ended as suddenly as it had begun. Questions, barbed as fishhooks, caught at her and pulled her back to earth, to winter, to James.

Why did James still wet the bed? He didn't do it every night, but why did he do it at all? Why couldn't he get himself all the way through dressing without her help? Why did he chew his nails?

Laurel bunched up her hands under the covers. Her own nails were bitten ragged. Perhaps James was not so different, after all.

But surely he should be able to go back and forth to school by himself by this time!

Barbara West's face came between Laurel and the darkness. She thumped over in bed. She did not want to remember it all again. It had not really been James's fault anyway. Probably she and Barbara would never have been friends.

Barbara had come to Riverside the April before. On that very first day, while the teacher was introducing her to the class, Laurel had felt there was something special about this small-boned, fair girl with the quiet, shy face, something that would have meaning for Laurel. Then Barbara had been given the desk across the aisle from hers and Laurel had discovered that the Wests had bought a house in the next block. Their friendship had seemed as sure as the coming spring.

Laurel loaned Barbara an eraser. They exchanged smiles. But that was as far as it went. Laurel thought of things to say — but lacked the courage to say them. Beginning a friendship was harder than Laurel had imagined.

Then the two of them had managed to walk out of the Girls' door side by side one noon hour. The sun, shining on streets still wet from an April shower, had been dazzling and Laurel could still remember the chorus of joyful bird-song.

"I guess we go the same way," Barbara had ventured. "We could walk together, if you like."

Laurel's heart had shot up like a rocket. Then she had remembered James waiting at the other door.

"No, I can't," she had blurted. Her voice had had a fierceness she did not mean. It hid her disappointment and Barbara, hearing only the anger, looked away, her face reddening.

"I can explain," Laurel had thought wildly. "If I tell her about James, she'll understand . . ."

But before she could find words, before she had been able to discover whether there were any words to find, Mary Lou Webster had happened by.

"Coming my way, Barb?" she had called lightly.

Mary Lou was older and usually walked with her own crowd of friends.

"Sure," Barbara said — and went.

That had been eight months ago. Mary Lou had only been intrigued by Barbara's newness. She had forgotten the younger girl in a matter of days. Once again, Barbara had no special friend.

Yet Laurel had never found another moment when an explanation would have been possible. She was almost sure that Barbara deliberately avoided being alone with her. And when she tried to plan what she would say if Barbara's attitude changed, Laurel still could not think of words which would explain James.

She imagined herself using her mother's words.

"He's still just a baby."

But Barbara would see for herself that James was nearly eight.

Or suppose she tried Dad's "He's lazy. He needs discipline, that's all."

What did laziness have to do with not being able to find your way to and from school?

Barbara would probably scoff at both of these attempts to explain. Laurel wondered unhappily if Mama and Daddy believed what they said themselves.

Laurel had tried to help James with his reading. He still did not know the words in his first preprimer. He read by reciting what he had learned off by heart or by guessing wildly from the pictures. Laurel had struggled to make him learn. She could make James do many things he did not want to do but even she had failed to force him to read.

She was getting nowhere. Laurel jerked her thoughts to a standstill. After all, other children had failed first grade. A boy in her own class, Malcolm Trevor, bragged about failing first grade. He got along fine now. Mama and Daddy must know. They were grown up.

She lay very still. James was sleeping soundly. The small, steady, up-and-down noise of his breathing comforted her, for no good reason.

She yawned hugely, turned over once more — and was asleep herself.

2

Trouble Multiplies

"Lindsay, stop making faces and eat your cereal or we'll all be late," Mama ordered.

"I'm not Lindsay. I'm an alligator — and I have a long jaw," Lindsay explained.

Mama returned sharply, "Don't talk nonsense," and Laurel looked at her in surprise. Mama usually thought Lindsay's "nonsense" was funny.

"Are you sure you're all right, Mama?" she asked. "Are you sure you didn't really hurt yourself when you fell?"

Mama did smile then but her face still had a tight, strained look.

"What a worrywart you are, Laurel," she said, as she had said a hundred times before when Laurel fussed without good reason. "I didn't really fall at all. I jumped."

That was true enough. Mama had been standing on a

kitchen chair to reach the spare light bulbs which were stowed away at the back of the top shelf. Lindsay, racing through on her way to breakfast, had slammed into the chair. Mama, about to climb down, had been off-balance already and when the chair toppled, she had jumped backwards and landed upright but with a thud that rattled the dishes. Mama had clutched at the counter top and stayed standing but she had clearly been in pain.

"What fool thing did you do now?" Dad had asked, coming to investigate. Laurel had heard Dad tell Mama more than once not to climb on chairs. She had a step stool with rubberized treads especially made for reaching things down from high shelves. So when Mama moved gingerly away from the counter and insisted that nothing had happened and she was fine, none of the children had told on her. They all knew that Mama didn't stop to think of things like step stools when she was in a hurry. She just reached for the nearest chair.

While Laurel studied her mother's face, trying to decide whether or not to worry, James was admiring Lindsay's imitation of an alligator. He put down his spoon and watched as his younger sister tried to eat with her chin sticking out as far as possible in the air.

"She's an alligator," he told the rest of the family.

Forgetting about Mama, Laurel scowled at James but she was too late. He had gone off into peals of laughter. He rocked back and forth on his chair.

"I'm an alligator too," he claimed, trying to stick his chin out as interestingly as Lindsay was doing.

"He's being a copycat again," Lindsay said immediately in her ordinary voice.

"You can be a crocodile," Laurel told James. He stopped laughing and looked at her. "They're the same thing almost," she said, "but hurry up and finish. I have to be at school on time."

Dad's newspaper crackled sharply as he folded it up and pushed it away from him.

"James is plenty old enough to get to school on his own," he said.

Laurel waited for Mama to explain but her mother said only, "James, that's enough. And, Lindsay, alligator or not, you and I have to be on our way in exactly four minutes."

Mama took Lindsay to nursery school on her way to work. Both Lindsay's school and the store where Mama worked were close enough to walk to but they were in the opposite direction to the school Laurel and James attended.

John Ross stuck to his point. "Laurel, are you still taking him to and from school every day?"

"He'd get lost if I didn't," Laurel said, not looking at James.

"I would not get lost," James argued loudly. "I know the way perfectly."

He was afraid and Laurel knew it. There were two big streets to cross on the way and there were three turnings. But Dad did not seem to hear the note of panic in his son's words. He stood up, grinned at James and ruffled up his hair.

"James is all right!" he said. "If you and your mother

would stop making a baby out of him, he'd get along fine. Get a move on, young fellow. You're walking to school yourself today."

James crumbled his toast in his fingers and looked frantically at Laurel but she still looked the other way. Their father, apparently unaware of the storm he had stirred up, left the room. He was a dentist with an office in the new clinic downtown.

"Susan, where's that manila envelope I brought home last night?" he called back from the hall.

"Sit right there until you've finished, Laurel Ross," Mama said, reading her daughter's thoughts. She got up then to go and help her husband. Laurel's eyes widened as she saw Mama's fingers grip the table edge as she got up and there was something wrong with the way she walked. She wasn't quite limping but . . .

"It's all right. I have it," Dad shouted. The front door opened. "See you tonight, Sue. I'm late now."

He was gone. And Laurel was finished. Anger surged up in her. She banged her chair back from the table, ran upstairs, jammed her books together into an untidy bundle, clattered back down, grabbed her coat from the hall closet, bent to yank on her boots and, without bothering to put on her mittens, had the door open.

"Making a baby out of him indeed," her thoughts churned. "Well . . . just wait. James will never make it alone. Never! When he gets lost, I hope that teaches Dad, once and for all . . ."

She was about to slam the door behind her when she

heard James call. She checked, in spite of herself, and turned and looked back.

Her little brother was running down the hall after her. He had jam smeared across one cheek and a ring of milk around his mouth. He had his coat on but not fastened. He was carrying his boots. But it was the look in his eyes that made her wait after all.

A new anger invaded her heart as she got him ready. She could have gone to school all by herself. She might even have met Barbara West and walked with her. She could have been early for once instead of arriving as the five-to-nine bell rang.

She scrubbed James's face with a hard hand. She thrust his feet into his boots and zipped up his coat so quickly that the zipper nipped his chin. James stood uncomplaining but Laurel did not relent until she was shoving him ahead of her down the front walk. Looking down, she saw his eyes shining with tears.

"You could learn the way," she said suddenly as they walked along together. "There's an easier way to go. It's a bit longer but you could probably manage it by yourself."

He clutched at her hand and she added, impatiently but gently, "Silly, I wouldn't let you go by yourself until I was sure you knew the way."

Laurel worked hard all morning. She could not afford to think about James in school. Laurel Ross had the highest marks in her class, but it took concentration and hard work. At noon, she raced to the door where she collected James and started for home. She hesitated for an instant, remem-

bering her decision to begin teaching him the easier route but she shook her head. There just was not time at noon.

Mrs. Birch had lunch waiting for them when they arrived.

"What rosy cheeks!" she exclaimed as they stamped the snow off their boots.

Laurel glowered. Every single solitary day, now that winter had come, Mrs. Birch told her what rosy cheeks she had. And Laurel knew that her cheeks were not rosy. Although the wind was really cold, neither Laurel nor James had more than a faint flush across their cheekbones.

"And what rosy cheeks you have, my darling," Mrs. Birch went on as Lindsay flew up the walk with a new drawing clutched in her mittened hand. The words meant something this time for Lindsay's cheeks positively glowed.

As they sat down to lunch, Lindsay spilled out an account of her morning. James and Laurel ate silently. Every so often Mrs. Birch looked at them uneasily. She had been keeping house for their mother ever since Mrs. Ross had taken a job in a children's clothing store owned and operated by one of her friends. Mrs. Ross worked through the noon hour, taking her lunch with her. She had arranged to finish at three-thirty so she could be home when the children got in from school. She had had the job for nearly two years and, at first, Lindsay had been at home all day. Even now, she only went to school in the mornings. She and Mrs. Birch were fast friends, but the older children still baffled Mrs. Birch.

"I just can't seem to make the other two out somehow,"

she had confided in Mama not long ago. Mama had sighed. She too found Lindsay much the easiest to understand.

That afternoon, Laurel did not get out of school promptly at four. The last period was home economics and Miss Marsden suggested that those who had time could remain to finish the aprons they were making. Laurel was sure it would only take her a minute, five at the most. James would wait that long. But then she had to wait her turn at the machine and Miss Marsden held her up discussing how well Laurel was working. It was impossible to explain to Miss Marsden about James. It was simpler just to stand and smile and nod and say "Thank you." At last, the teacher grew aware of the girl's restlessness. She frowned slightly and said coolly, "All right, Laurel, run along."

Laurel turned miserably away. Trying not to think about it, she got into her coat and boots and went to look for James. When she reached the door where they always met, he was nowhere to be seen.

"Do you know where James Ross is?" she asked a small group of children playing in the schoolyard.

Some shook their heads. Two or three just stood there. One boy put in, "We didn't do it."

"Do what?" Laurel questioned sharply.

But the little boy stood and refused to answer.

"He went that way," one of the others volunteered at last. Then they dashed away from her and grew terribly busy playing Fox and Geese.

Laurel began to run down the street the child had

pointed out. She was nearly halfway home before she found him. She did not know him at first. He was lying in the snow. He was covered with snow. It had been rubbed in his hair and stuffed down his shirt. His cap was missing. His reader, the preprimer she had tried to help him to read, had been torn to bits. The pages, with their cheerful, unreal pictures of perfect children, were scattered over the road and the neighboring yards. His glasses, miraculously still in one piece, were half buried in a nearby drift. His cheek was bruised and he had a cut over one eye. He was crying, but it was a strange inhuman cry like nothing Laurel had heard before.

"James," she shouted, bending over him in an agony of fear, "James! James!"

He did not seem to know her. The thin, lost sound went on and on. She knelt down in the snow beside him. She grabbed his shoulders and shook him.

"James, stop it. It's me. It's Laurel!"

Suddenly, he saw her and clutched at her with frantic hands. Holding onto her for dear life, he began to cry in earnest. Immediately, Laurel felt better.

"What happened?" she demanded.

But he could not tell her. She had to put the story together from bits and pieces. Some boys had come up to him after school.

"They said to go with them . . . they said you were waiting . . ." he sobbed.

Laurel cleaned off his glasses and shoved them back on his face. Then she gathered him up. She supported him with one hand and brushed the snow off him with the other. She managed to get him moving toward home although he was still crying.

Now, at last, her parents would understand, she thought, as she half pushed, half pulled him along and tried, at the same time, to keep a grip on her books. His book was left forgotten in the snow. Now Mama would have to talk about it. Now Dad would have to give in and do something . . .

But when they reached the house, after what seemed an interminable journey to Laurel, Mrs. Birch, who should have gone, was still there. She did not seem to see that James needed instant care. She was full of the excitement and bustling with the importance of being the bearer of bad news.

"Your mother has broken her hip," she announced in a voice which sounded deafeningly loud to Laurel. "I'm to take charge of things till she's better. My, what a day this has been!"

"Yes," Laurel said.

If it had been anybody but Mrs. Birch, she would have broken down but Mrs. Birch would never understand. Something stubborn in Laurel knew that Mrs. Birch wanted her to cry, that the housekeeper would enjoy comforting her. Laurel knew better than to say another word. Her voice was knotted in her throat, aching and tight. She turned abruptly, took hold of James's hand and led him away. Mrs. Birch started after them but the phone rang and she went to answer it. Laurel got James upstairs and did the best she could. She cleaned him up. She put him to bed. She tucked his toy bear in with him although she had been telling him he was too old to sleep with a bear. Then she went down again. Mrs. Birch had only just hung up.

"You're a cool customer, I must say," she remarked, looking at the girl's still face. "Where's James?"

"I put him to bed. He has a cold," Laurel answered readily. It sounded like the truth as she said it.

"Will you be all right now then?" Mrs. Birch asked. She sounded really worried but whether she was anxious about the Rosses or about having been kept late, Laurel was not sure. "My husband's brother and his family are coming to spend the weekend with us. I phoned and told Al what had happened and he said he'd get things going. But, if you'll be all right, I'll run along. Your Dad should be home any minute. I promised him I'd come on Monday and stay for supper after this till your Mum's home."

"How long will Mama be away?" Laurel asked.

"I don't know," Mrs. Birch admitted, but then she sighed heavily and shook her head. "I should think it would be months," she said. Laurel's face whitened but the housekeeper did not notice. She looked at her watch again.

"We'll be fine," Laurel said. "You go ahead."

Mrs. Birch patted her shoulder, issued some last minute instructions and bustled off. Laurel watched her from the door. But she was not thinking of Mrs. Birch at all. She was thinking of Aunt Jessica.

3

How Did Mama
Manage?

Not certain when to expect their father, the two
girls sat down to supper at six-thirty without him.
Both of them were relieved when they heard him at the
door before Laurel had finished asking the blessing. Lindsay, not waiting for "Amen," jumped from her place and
ran to him. Laurel sat, her hands scrunched together in her
lap, and waited. But Dad did not swing Lindsay up onto
his shoulder this time.

"Easy does it, Linnet," he said. "Let me get my coat off.
Where's your sister? At the table! Then what are you
doing out here? I'll bet Laurel didn't excuse you."

He shepherded the small girl ahead of him through the
living room. When he caught sight of Laurel sitting alone,
he asked at once, "Where's James?"

"He has a cold," Laurel explained. The words came with

more difficulty this time. Her voice creaked oddly. Mama would have wondered what was wrong at once, but Dad was different. He listened without expression as she built up the lie with convincing details. "His throat is getting sore. I made him go to bed. He felt a bit hot. I'll take him something to eat after."

John Ross nodded and pulled his chair to the table. Lindsay, her napkin anchored once again beneath her chin, opened her mouth to argue but a look from Laurel silenced her.

The little girl studied her older sister thoughtfully. Then she took a big bite of the macaroni and cheese Mrs. Birch had left ready for them. She mumbled, her mouth still full, "James hates macaroni."

"I'll take him some soup," Laurel said.

"I hate macaroni too," Lindsay tried.

"You do not!" Laurel began indignantly. Then she settled for, "Well, just leave what you don't want."

Lindsay smiled like a cat who has managed to steal cream. John Ross was never one to catch the undertones in his children's conversation. He was tired and worried and he heard nothing out of the ordinary in the exchange between the two girls. He had no idea of what had happened between them in James's room half an hour earlier so he could not know that Lindsay was blackmailing Laurel right under his very nose.

In spite of her hurry to be gone, it had taken Mrs. Birch an eternity to leave. Laurel had stood stolidly under a deluge of good advice and last minute reminders although she actually made little sense of them. She was far too troubled about James. When the door closed behind the housekeeper, Laurel waited only long enough to be sure the woman was really gone before she flew for the stairs.

Then she halted abruptly and changed her course. A hot-water bottle was the thing James needed! He had shivered so when she had helped him to undress and his teeth had chattered frighteningly. When she herself had been shivery with flu, Mama had tucked a hot-water bottle into bed with her and Laurel had warmed her icy feet against it. She had found it so comforting, so cozy . . . It took her awhile to find where Mama kept it and then she had to wait for the water to run hot before she filled it.

"James," she had said, bursting through the door into his room, "did you think I was never coming . . ."

Then she had seen them. Lindsay was sitting cross-legged on the foot of his bed. She was telling him something, some joke which Laurel never heard, for Lindsay stopped the instant her big sister appeared. But James went on giggling. The covers were thrown back. The teddy bear, which he had hugged so desperately such a short time ago, was lying face down on the floor.

When she was calmer, after Lindsay had been sent packing and James was back under a mountain of blankets with his bear and his hot-water bottle, Laurel tried to forget losing her temper. She tried to forget James saying, in a bewildered voice, "But I don't have a cold." And Lindsay asking saucily, "What's his tempercher? Mama always takes our tempercher."

But none of that mattered now, she told herself shortly. James was cowed and Lindsay was not going to tell. Not that there was anything to tell really! Probably James did have a cold! He had been chilled right through when she found him.

What mattered now was her mother.

"Dad," she began.

"Laurel," he said at the same moment.

Laurel hushed and listened. Later she would explain about Mrs. Birch being the wrong person and about James's "cold" and surely Dad would think himself of sending for Aunt Jessica.

"I don't know what to do," Dad said anxiously. "I have a meeting at seven-thirty. Mrs. Birch stayed as long as she could but she had some of her family coming . . ."

"Yes, I know," Laurel put in.

"Your mother wouldn't like you to be left alone," he went on. "I don't know where I'd find a baby-sitter now. Usually Mrs. Birch is available. But if James is really sick . . ."

Under Lindsay's straight gaze, Laurel told part of the truth.

"He's not really very sick," she said. "I can look after him all right. But, Dad, what really happened to Mama?"

"It was a freak accident," Dad said tiredly. "She somehow managed to fracture her hip right here this morning, climbing after something. But she kept on walking until she caught her heel on the edge of one of those hot air registers at the store. I think she must have been dragging the one foot a bit. And she disimpacted the fracture and she just plain couldn't stand up again."

"But she didn't even fall down this morning!" Laurel protested, her eyes wide. "She jumped . . ."

"So she told me, but not at the time," Dad said wryly. "Perhaps if we'd known earlier . . . Listen, girls, it's five after seven. I'm supposed to be at the meeting early. I don't suppose, Laurel, that you could manage for a little . . . There's Lindsay to put to bed and these dishes . . . and your homework. But I promised Douglas MacNab I'd be there to go over the financial side with him . . . and I'd like to drop in again at the hospital."

"I can manage," Laurel said stoutly. Then, meeting her small sister's gaze squarely, she added, "Lindsay's big enough to help. She can get herself ready for bed."

Lindsay grinned at her. For a moment, they were friends.

John Ross sighed with relief and pushed back his chair.

"Well, if you think you can," he said. "It will only be this once. Mrs. Birch will be here on Monday. I won't be late. I'll get away as soon as I can."

"Daddy, couldn't we ask Aunt Jessica to come?" Laurel burst out as her father rose and turned to leave them.

"Jessica . . ." he said vaguely. "I suppose I should call Jessica and let her know. Her number's there, Laurel. Could you . . . ?"

A car horn honked outside.

"That'll be Douglas," he explained unnecessarily. "Forget about Jessica, Laurel. Forget about the dishes too. Just take care of the children and I'll be home as early as I can."

He was gone.

The two girls sat and looked at each other.

"We didn't have dessert," Lindsay said finally.

Laurel cleared away their plates and found some applesauce and cookies.

"Laurel," Lindsay said suddenly, "Miss Deeping can figure skate."

"Miss Deeping . . ." Laurel echoed blankly.

Lindsay helped herself to another cookie. It was her third and she was only allowed two but Laurel kept quiet.

"Miss Deeping's my teacher, stupid . . ." Lindsay told her sister. "James doesn't want to stay in bed," she went on. She then crammed the cookie in her hand into her mouth in a way that would have scandalized her mother and reached for one more.

"Never you mind James — and that's enough cookies," Laurel said sharply. "You'd better go upstairs and get undressed."

All at once, Lindsay's eyes flooded with tears.

"I want Mama!" she wailed.

Laurel looked at her helplessly. This forlorn child was not the impertinent, cocksure Lindsay she knew. She got up and went around the table to her.

"Well, you can't have her, so come on," she said, not unkindly. "I'll read you a story after your bath."

Lindsay cried quietly all the way up the stairs. Laurel saw her through her bath, read her three stories, sang her one song and then another. Finally she had to leave although Lindsay began to cry again. She left the light on in her little sister's room and went down and prepared a tray for James.

When she got upstairs with it, she found Lindsay in bed with her brother. The little girl was wide awake. James sat up at once and began to gobble the food Laurel had brought to him. Laurel opened her mouth to order Lindsay back to her own bed. But something warned her that the moment she went down to tackle the dishes, Lindsay would scurry right back into James's room. Laurel looked at the two of them sternly.

"If I let you stay in here, Lindsay, will you be quiet and go right to sleep?" she demanded.

The younger children's eyes shone. They nodded solemnly. Laurel removed James's tray to the dresser and lingered for a moment, but the two of them lay so still and straight in the bed and looked so full of good intentions that at last she went downstairs.

Ever since she could remember, Laurel Ross had helped with the dishes. But never before had she had to see to all the clearing up after a meal by herself. It had been a long and difficult day. How did Mama ever manage? As she started to carry the dishes out to the kitchen, she heard her own footsteps making a lonely, too loud sound in the empty rooms. What was she to do with the leftover macaroni? What was to be done with two slices of tomato? Lindsay had left most of her milk.

Suddenly, Laurel saw that she had left the burner on under the pot in which she had heated the soup for James. She snatched at it without thinking and yelped as it burned her hand.

Things went from bad to worse. Her hand stung horribly when she plunged it into the hot dishwater. The phone rang three times before she had the dishes washed.

Each time it was a friend of Mama's who had just heard the news.

"Can I do anything to help, Laurel?" one of them asked.

"No, thank you. We're okay," Laurel answered, trying to keep her voice steady.

If only Mrs. Webster would just COME. But Mrs. Webster was on her way to a concert. Mrs. Marcus promised to bring over a pie the next day. Mrs. Bates was going to the hospital to visit her mother-in-law and she would inquire about Mama while she was there. (Laurel was thankful Mrs. Bates had not offered to come. She was forever clutching children to her and calling them "kiddies.")

Laurel dragged herself back to the sink. She was nearly done. She only had to get the casserole clean. She tried not to notice how dark everything looked outside the window over the sink. Maybe Dad would come home in a minute. She bent her head over the casserole and scrubbed at it.

"Crash!"

Laurel leapt like a startled deer when the great thud sounded above her head. The casserole, which she had had braced on the edge of the sink, flew from her shaking hands and smashed to smithereens on the floor. It was Mama's new Corningware that she had been given for her birthday in September.

"Thump!"

Laurel ran for the stairs. Her brother and sister were on the floor, fighting tooth and nail. Laurel dragged them apart.

"I thought you promised you'd go to sleep," she hissed at Lindsay.

"He kicked me!" Lindsay shrilled.

"She kicked me first," James yelled right after her.

Laurel grabbed Lindsay by one arm and jerked her roughly to her feet. "You go to your own room this minute," she ordered.

Lindsay pulled free and stood her ground, glaring up at the sister who towered over her. "You're not my mother," she shouted. "I don't have to do what you say."

"Get into that bed," Laurel thundered at James.

James did as he was told. He was used to obeying Laurel. But Lindsay did not budge. Laurel stared down at her. The little girl's eyes were enormous. Her cheeks blazed with color. Her chin was thrust out defiantly.

"I can do what I like, so there!" she hurled at the older girl.

Laurel slapped her. She slapped her right across the cheek and she slapped her hard. Lindsay's courage crumbled. Bursting into tears, she ran away from the other two into her own room. Laurel heard the door slam. Through the closed door, she could still hear Lindsay sobbing bitterly, "Mama! Mama!" Her hand, the hand she had already burned, now smarted from the slap she had given her sister.

"You made Lindsay cry," James said.

Laurel did not answer. She went away from them, down the stairs again. She did not cry but she moved stiffly like a wind-up toy. She had taken all she could.

"Phone Aunt Jessica," a voice inside her was saying. It didn't sound like her own voice. "Just phone Aunt Jessica."

4

A Call for Help

It was as though Laurel were walking in a dream. Her feet felt heavy and faraway. It took her several minutes to locate her aunt's telephone number although it was written in the front of the phone book. She dialed slowly. She had never made a long distance call before. There were so many numbers. She dialed one and then looked for the next. After she dialed the last number, there was a short silence and then a clicking sound. Even from where she sat, she could still hear Lindsay crying. Or was she imagining it? She wondered dully if James were crying too. Then the phone began to ring. Aunt Jessica picked it up on the fourth ring.

"Hello," she said briskly.

Laurel just sat.

"Hello . . ." Aunt Jessica said again. Her voice had a question in it now.

"Aunt Jessica, it's me . . . it's Laurel," Laurel began.

The voice, coming across so many miles and yet sounding so near, warmed and softened at once. "Why, Laurel, what is it?"

Then Laurel did begin to cry. She cried every bit as hard as her four-year-old sister.

"Laurel . . . Laurel!" Aunt Jessica tried to reach her, to calm her. "Tell me. Stop crying, Laurel, and tell me what's wrong."

The story came out. Jessica Marlowe did not understand much of it. She got the fact that her sister Susan was in the hospital with a broken hip. She understood that Laurel had burned her hand and slapped Lindsay. There was something about James being knocked into the snow and his not being able to read, something about a broken dish, something about Mrs. Birch coming every day. As Laurel gulped out bits and pieces, Jessica tried to put them together but it was no use. She did know that she herself had grown concerned about James during the last two or three visits she had made with her sister's family. She had always known that Mrs. Birch was not the right person to be taking care of the older children. Most of all, she knew a call for help — and Jessica Marlowe could never resist such a cry. It would be awkward but she would manage. Her mind started sorting through the possibilities.

"Laurel," she said firmly, when she was sure the girl was paying attention, "we'll be there tomorrow. Can you manage until tomorrow afternoon?"

"Tomorrow," Laurel echoed — and some of the courage which had kept her going so far returned. "Yes, Aunt Jessica," she said, in a voice not too different from her usual one. "I can manage till tomorrow."

"Good girl," Aunt Jessica said.

It was not until Laurel had hung up the receiver and was just sitting there, feeling rescued, that she remembered that Aunt Jessica would not be coming alone. She would be bringing Elspeth with her.

Laurel remembered Elspeth and the next minute forgot her. Aunt Jessica was coming. That was all that really mattered. Aunt Jessica would see to everything, Mrs. Birch included. Aunt Jessica might even understand about James.

Laurel, suddenly, unexpectedly, giggled. Wait till Dad heard Aunt Jessica was arriving tomorrow! Dad had been known to call Aunt Jessica "the Avenging Angel!" Mama had scolded him for saying it in the children's hearing but she had smiled, all the same. Aunt Jessica had a way of tidying everything in sight. It was strange to think of Mama and Aunt Jessica as sisters. Of course, Aunt Jessica was the older. Maybe that was what made her boss Mama sometimes as though Mama were no older than Lindsay. Mama left things in a comfortable clutter. Books piled up on top of the piano. Gloves and scarves and letters jumbled together in a heap on the hall table. The house was not dirty but, as Mama said, it definitely had a "lived-in look." Aunt Jessica would have everything polished and put away within twenty-four hours. "Relax, woman," Dad would growl at her.

Laurel liked Aunt Jessica's orderliness. Mama often

shook her head over Laurel, who kept her room neat as a pin. "You'd think you were Jessica's daughter and Elspeth were mine," she'd say.

Laurel was still sitting by the phone, lost in thought, when she heard the front door open. Like an arrow loosed from a bow, she sped to her father.

"How's Mama?" she questioned, her voice squeaking with tension.

"She's all right," her father said. "They've given her something for the pain and they're going to operate first thing in the morning. She was pretty sleepy but she sent her love."

Then Laurel admitted to herself how desperately lonely she had been as she struggled with the younger children and with the dishes. All through the troubles which had beset her, even during the moments when she was spilling everything out to Aunt Jessica, she had been worrying about and wanting Mama.

She drew a deep quivering breath which was almost a sob. Dad put his hand on her shoulder in an unaccustomed gesture and gave her a little loving shake.

"Really, Laurel, she's going to be fine," he reassured her. "We'll have her home again in six weeks or so. Are Lindsay and James asleep?"

"I'll go and check," Laurel said, turning away so that he could no longer see her face. Six weeks! and she knew she was too young to be allowed even to visit her mother in the hospital.

The two little ones were both sleeping. Lindsay had her arm over her eyes. Laurel stood for a moment beside her bed but there was nothing she could do now. "I'm sorry," she whispered, knowing Lindsay could not hear the words.

Then she went back down to her father. When she reached the hall, she saw the clock in the living room. Her eyes widened in disbelief. It was not even nine o'clock. She felt as though she had been alone for years but really it had been less than two hours. Dad was sitting in the big chair by the fireplace. He was holding the newspaper but he lowered it as she came through the door.

"How did you get along?" he asked.

This time there were no tears. She told him she had put the other two to bed and had done the dishes. She did not tell him about slapping Lindsay or about breaking the casserole. He was not the sort of person you told such things to. She did show him her burned hand although she would not have done so had her mother been home. She had smeared some ointment on it while she was upstairs.

"Is it very sore?" he asked.

"Not very," Laurel told him, although it was throbbing as she spoke.

"It looks all right," he said doubtfully.

"Mama would say 'Keep it up,'" Laurel responded to the uncertainty in his voice with a sureness she did not really feel. "And it says 'For burns' on the stuff I put on it. I phoned Aunt Jessica. She's coming tomorrow."

"Coming here?"

Laurel nodded. She was the uncertain one now. Her father looked taken aback and not wholly pleased. At last, he smiled. There was a wryness to his smile but Laurel was able to relax again.

"Trust Jessica to rally around," was all he said. Then he wanted to know further details — when the Marlowes would arrive and how long they planned to stay. "Never mind," he said, when Laurel admitted she did not know. "I'll call her and get it all straight. You'd better get along to bed now."

She went to the kitchen first and picked up the pieces of the casserole. She wiped the counter off tidily, flicked off the light and started for the stairs.

Her father's voice came after her.

"I'd like a kiss," he said.

She rushed to him then and he gathered her onto his lap. It had been a long time since Laurel had sat on her father's knee. Lindsay did still and, once in a while, James, but Laurel discovered that she remembered exactly where to rest her head in the crook of his shoulder. The scrape of his cheek against hers and the smell of his shaving lotion were just as they had always been.

"I used to walk the floor with you when you were a baby," he claimed.

Laurel doubted it but she laughed all the same. Mama often said that he had never even wakened when they howled as infants. And she had never seen him walk the floor with Lindsay. Still, he was hers, wonderfully hers, and he was here when she needed him. She drowsed, so tired after everything that had happened that, suddenly, her thoughts began to slide away out of reach.

"None of that," Dad said, over her head. "Up to bed with you."

He rose with her and steadied her until she was awake enough to navigate alone.

She looked back from the doorway but he had disappeared behind his paper.

The next morning took care of itself. Mrs. Webster came over and helped Laurel get the lunch. Mrs. Marcus delivered her pie and took Lindsay home to play with Joan. James sat and watched television all morning. By this time, he believed he really had the cold Laurel had claimed he had. He would not go out to play.

When the phone rang at eleven o'clock, Laurel thought it would be someone else calling to find out how Mama was. People had been calling all morning. Laurel had never realized before how many friends Mama had. But it was Barbara West.

"Would you like a hamster?" she began abruptly as soon as she heard Laurel's "Hello."

"A hamster!" Laurel repeated.

She knew, of course, that Barbara had hamsters — nine of them. Every child on the street had been over to the Wests to see the eight babies soon after they were born. They had been incredibly tiny and pink and helpless. Laurel had gone along with Lindsay to look, hoping that she might get a chance to talk to Barbara by herself. But there were far too many children milling about for any private conversation. She had not had the courage to go back since. Lindsay, however, was a fast friend of the child who lived next door to the Wests and she had kept the Rosses up-to-date on the Wests' hamsters. They had grown. They had fur. Half of them were white and half golden. Barbara was going to keep every single one of them. Barbara was "mad about animals," Lindsay had said, quoting Mrs. West.

"Are you there, Laurel?"

"Yes," Laurel said, "but I don't think I can have a hamster."

"You've *got* to take one," Barbara insisted, sounding entirely unlike herself. "My mother says I have to get homes for them all today or she'll give them to the Humane Society. They got loose last night," she explained. Her voice had dropped almost to a whisper on the last words. Laurel had a vision of Mrs. West chasing eight baby hamsters around the house at night and she laughed.

"It's not funny," Barbara snapped. "We're still missing one. Please, Laurel, ask your mother. I'll bet she'll say 'Yes.' "

Laurel explained about Mama.

"I guess I could ask Aunt Jessica though when she gets here," she finished dubiously.

"Ask her," Barbara ordered. "And call me back. I still have four to find places for . . . if we find that other one."

Laurel hung up and returned to the kitchen. Mrs. Webster laughed.

"That was Barbara West, wasn't it?" she asked. "She called Mary Louise at eight-thirty this morning!"

Laurel fought down the hurt inside. If Barbara had called Mary Lou at eight-thirty, she had been calling other people for two-and-a-half hours before she phoned the Rosses! Laurel forgot that the other girl might not have spent all morning telephoning but probably had put in a good part of it searching the house for the one missing hamster.

"Are you letting Mary Lou have one?"

"I am not!" Mrs. Webster said emphatically. "We already have three cats. How much chance would a hamster have with three felines lying in wait for him?"

Laurel could see what she meant. She was sure Aunt Jessica would be just as emphatic even though the Rosses had no pets at all.

Mrs. Webster sighed. "That Mary Louise is daft about animals," she complained. "She brought home a stray dog last week. I thought the cats would murder him before I could persuade her to let me take him to the Humane Society. She and Barbara are two of a kind. Rachel says Alice is just the same. That's one real bond between the two girls."

"Alice who?" Laurel asked idly.

She knew Rachel was Mrs. West but she had never heard of anyone called Alice. She was only half listening for Mrs. Webster's answer . . . until it did not come. A small odd silence fell and when Laurel turned her head to look at the woman, Mrs. Webster looked embarrassed.

"She's just a relative of the Wests, dear," she said hastily. "Here, let me do that. You're taking off too much peeling."

Laurel wondered briefly about the mysterious Alice but, with the Marlowes coming, she had more important things to think about.

The Marlowes arrived at three. The trunk was crammed

with luggage and the back seat of the car was heaped high.

"It's all arranged, John," Aunt Jessica said as she and Dad went up the walk together. "Miss Whitcomb gave me leave of absence till after Christmas and Elspeth can go to school with Laurel for the rest of this term. Susan should be home from the hospital by January."

Elspeth said nothing at all. She trailed into the house and just stood in the hall letting suitcases and boxes pile up around her. Laurel, struggling with an armload of dresses which had been hanging in plastic bags in the back of the car, shot her an exasperated look. Why couldn't she go and put her own things away?

Suddenly Laurel wondered where Elspeth was going to sleep. Aunt Jessica had disappeared up the stairs with Dad. She was walking back and forth from room to room. Laurel hurried up, but it was settled when she got there. Elspeth was moving in with her. Lindsay was to have James's small room in the gable. James was going to move downstairs with their father and Aunt Jessica would sleep in Lindsay's room.

"Aunt Jessica —" Laurel protested.

But Aunt Jessica was not listening. She was beginning to move Lindsay's clothes out of the closet.

"James . . ." Laurel thought. "James will be frightened."

She ran back down the stairs. She must catch her father and make him understand that James needed her to look after him. She must prevent Aunt Jessica from telling James that he was going to be moved.

But she was too late again. James was in Dad's room with their father. Through the open door, Laurel could see him. His usually sallow cheeks were pink with pleasure.

"Just us men," he was saying proudly, echoing his father's words. "Just us men."

Laurel turned and stalked across the hall. There was Elspeth, still standing, still waiting.

"You can take your stuff upstairs and dump it in my room," Laurel told her harshly.

Elspeth came out of the dream world she had been in and stared at her cousin. Laurel grabbed her coat out of the hall closet.

"If anybody asks you, tell them I had to go and get something," she said. "I won't be long."

With that, she was out the door and running up the street to Barbara's.

5

Puff

"I only have one left," Barbara said. "Besides the mother, I mean. Mother says I can keep her."

She did not explain that when they had finally found the last errant young hamster sitting very still under the laundry tubs, her mother had weakened enough to say, "If nobody claims him, I suppose we might keep him too . . . but if someone else wants him, Barbara, you're to hand him over." Barbara had been hoping against hope nobody would come. Disappointment made her sound ungracious and Laurel drew back into her shell. She stood her ground, however, and said:

"I do want him. It's all right."

"I thought you said your aunt wouldn't let you have him," Barbara stalled.

"Of course, she'll let me." Laurel lied quickly, her face

suddenly warm. "If she'd said 'no,' do you think I'd be here?"

Barbara did not protest any further. She led the way silently.

"There," she said, pointing.

"Oh," Laurel breathed.

She had not expected him to be so round and soft-looking, so small and real and altogether miraculous.

Barbara reached into the cage and caught him.

"You really shouldn't bother them in the daytime," she said. "They sometimes bite when they're half asleep. Here . . ."

She put him gently into Laurel's cupped hands. He stayed curled up in a drowsy golden ball. He felt incredibly warm and alive against her palms. His minute feet half tickled her. He kept his eyes closed.

I'll call him Puff, Laurel thought.

Then he yawned. It was such an immense yawn for so tiny a creature that it startled Laurel. He looked, for an instant, like a pint-sized lion preparing to roar. Instead, he shut his mouth and went back to sleep.

As she stood there holding him, Laurel felt the hurt within her ease. She forgot the emptiness of the house with Mama gone. She forgot Elspeth standing in the hall and looking unapproachable. She forgot Aunt Jessica arranging everything to suit herself. She even forgot, for a moment, the excitement which she had seen glowing on James's face. All that was real now was this small sleepy golden hamster who was hers. She looked across at Barbara.

"I'll take him home right now," Laurel said.

For a second, she was aware of the misery which was tightening Barbara's face. All day, Barbara must have been saying good-bye to her beloved hamsters.

"His name is Butterball," Barbara stated.

Laurel forgot about Barbara's misery.

"I'm going to call him Puff," she told the other girl. "He doesn't know his name yet, does he?"

He was only a month old. Barbara hesitated. Then she shook her head, turned on her heel and led the way to the front door.

"I'll carry him inside my coat," Laurel said. "It's fleece-lined so he'll be warm."

It was the only thing she could do to make up. His name *was* Puff. She could not change that for Barbara or anyone.

"You *do* have everything ready for him?" Barbara said, as Laurel started out of the house with Puff tucked into the front of her jacket. "You have a cage and some food? He likes peanuts. And hamster food, of course. And apple."

Laurel stood still. She thought back. Did Barbara have an extra cage? . . . No, that was only the Wests' old rabbit hutch fixed over. What would she do with him if she didn't have a cage? But they did have apples at home, and she could put him in a box. She couldn't go home and face everything waiting for her there without Puff.

"Yes, I have all I'll need," she assured Barbara. "Thanks a lot," she added belatedly.

Barbara shivered in the doorway. Laurel said "Bye," and ran for home.

She stopped in front of the house and considered for a moment. Where would Aunt Jessica be? Probably still putting clothes away in Lindsay's room. She slipped through the front door as quietly as she could. James was in the hall.

"Laurie," he said. "I'm going to sleep with Daddy."

"Fine."

James was not so certain now. When Aunt Jessica had sent him downstairs with armloads of clothes, when he had trotted back up to the small room over the gable which had been his ever since he could remember and found Lindsay bouncing up and down in the middle of his bed while their aunt hung dresses in his closet, he had been filled with a sense of loss. Aunt Jessica made everything look so settled, so definite — and he could not find Laurel anywhere. Elspeth was the only one who seemed to know anything about Laurel's disappearance and she said shortly, "She's gone out." James had waited in the hall for her. She had just been gone about fifteen minutes but, to him, it had seemed forever. Yet now she was not even looking at him.

"Where's Aunt Jessica?" she demanded. She was almost whispering and there was something strange about her. She looked bunched up somehow. But James had been trained to answer rather than ask questions.

"She's unpacking her own things now," he told her.

"Thanks," Laurel said and hurried away from him, up the stairs, before he could find the words to stop her.

For once, Laurel was unaware of James and his problems. She turned right at the top of the stairs, scuttled down the short stretch of hall and opened her bedroom door. Elspeth was sitting facing her.

"Oh!" Laurel said. But she could not retreat.

"Is that you, Laurel?" Aunt Jessica called.

Laurel pulled Puff out of the front of her jacket and held him out to Elspeth.

"We'll have to hide him," she implored.

Elspeth came alive. She was on her feet and at the door before her mother reached it. "Hurry," she shot over her shoulder.

Laurel dove for the closet. There was a shoe box on the floor. She had no time to examine it. She stooped down and deposited Puff in it and turned to face her aunt. Elspeth had delayed her just long enough.

"Were you calling, Mother?" she had asked, poking her head around the door.

"Was that Laurel I heard?" her mother demanded and brushed past her daughter into the bedroom. The girls held their breath. The closet door stood open. Suppose Aunt Jessica wanted to make sure their clothes were hung up correctly? Suppose . . .

"What are you doing wearing that jacket indoors?" Aunt Jessica asked. Much to Laurel's relief, she did not wait for an answer. "It's perhaps a good thing. Elspeth, you get yours on too. Then the two of you can come out in the garage and help me bring up that extra bedstead for Elspeth."

Laurel followed immediately in her aunt's wake with Elspeth a close second. They were so efficient that Jessica Marlowe wondered what they were up to. Her sister Susan would have looked into matters right then and there, but Jessica was too occupied getting the household in order. When the two girls, usually as indolent as turtles, insisted that they could get the bedstead up to the room and assemble it and make the bed themselves, she was surprised but too grateful to question. Laurel and Elspeth struggled up the stairs with the bulky, slippery, heavy mattress. When they reached the room they were to share, they dropped it thankfully.

"The coast's clear," Elspeth whispered.

Laurel ran to the closet and bent over Puff's box. Then she saw that she had put him into an old box Lindsay had used to make a diorama. There was a window cut in one side and Puff was gone, leaving no trace.

6

The Little Monster

"He got away!" Laurel gasped.

They looked at each other wildly, the shock and dismay on their faces identical.

"Suppose Mother finds him!" Elspeth put what both of them were thinking into words. Then her mouth quirked up at the corners as she pictured her mother suddenly coming face-to-face with the hamster.

Laurel's answering grin was fleeting.

"She'd never let us keep him," she said despairingly. "We'll just have to find him ourselves — and fast!"

They began to hunt feverishly. Laurel found herself looking in highly improbable places — in her top dresser drawer, behind the books in the bookcase, even under her pillow.

As she searched, a part of her mind was trying to take in

an entirely new Elspeth, a girl she was certain she had never met before.

Elspeth looked so different, to begin with. Or maybe she, Laurel, had just never looked at her properly. Their grandmother Demming was forever singing Elspeth's praises when she visited in Riverside. (Laurel was to learn that when Gran visited the Marlowes, it was Laurel and Lindsay who were perfect.)

"Elspeth is so mature," Gran would say when Laurel had quarreled with Lindsay and the two of them had ended up in tears. "Elspeth keeps her hair so nicely, but of course, she has it done once a week," Gran would comment when Laurel's hair flopped into her eyes. Laurel had seen for herself what lovely clothes Elspeth possessed. When she and her mother came to visit, Elspeth seemed to delight in wearing outfits far grander than anything Laurel owned. She had no way of knowing that Elspeth envied Laurel her comfortable old clothes, that some of Elspeth's stiffness of manner was due to her feeling of being terribly overdressed when she stayed with the Rosses.

Elspeth went to a private school. She went there because her mother was private secretary to the headmistress. But Laurel, who until lately had loved boarding school stories with a passion, had visions of Elspeth involved in countless "midnight feasts" and surrounded by a bevy of friends.

Gran was fond of enumerating the prizes Elspeth had won, too. Although Elspeth was no better student than Laurel, she had earned countless prizes. In the large public school Laurel attended, prizes were given once a year. Laurel had stood at the top of her class twice and she had two books to prove it, but they did not begin to compare with Elspeth's tennis and badminton trophies, ribbons for swimming, plus far grander books than Laurel's two. Elspeth was even a prefect.

When she had visited the Rosses, Elspeth had always been polite. But she had also been distant and, Laurel was certain, terribly bored. Until today!

Laurel got up from peering into the dark cave under the bed and looked across at her cousin. Elspeth's velvet jumper was dusty. Her "hairdo," as Laurel had dubbed it for years, was disarranged. Her cheeks were pink. Her eyes were sparkling. She had come alive!

Elspeth found Laurel just as disconcerting. Laurel, the sulky girl who was so hard to talk to, the bossy girl Elspeth had thought impossible to live with, had disappeared. In her place was an ally.

"Girls! Laurel! Elspeth!"

They leapt guiltily and faced the door together. The wall of reserve between them had been toppled by a tiny hamster. They were as one. Aunt Jessica came sailing in, her forehead wrinkled, her mouth stern.

"Why, you've only brought the mattress up here! What on earth have you been doing? You came in with that half an hour ago," she began.

The girls shot past her.

"We're just going," they chorused, ignoring her questions. They dashed pell-mell down the stairs to fetch the rest of the bed.

Jessica Marlowe's tired mouth relaxed a little.

Elspeth seemed to be fitting in, after all, she thought

gratefully. She had been wondering whether she should relent and allow her daughter to return to Briarhill and board there during the weeks she would be with the Rosses.

Since Paul Marlowe's death five years before, Jessica and Elspeth had shared an apartment in Toronto. It was close to the school where Jessica worked and which Elspeth was permitted to attend as a day girl. This time, Elspeth had begged to stay at the school but, impulsively, Jessica had determined to take her daughter with her. Elspeth was too lonely, too shut up in herself, too grown-up for her own good. Being part of a family for a while might help.

Jessica Marlowe thought of her daughter's face as she had just seen it. Obviously the two girls were up to something. Elspeth had looked years younger. Well, perhaps not years exactly, but younger and decidedly happier.

"She's been so bored lately," her mother sighed. Then she remembered the girl who had flown past her and clattered down the stairs after her cousin. Her mother smiled, shrugged her shoulders at the hope that warmed her, and went down to the kitchen to see about supper.

"We have to find him," Laurel hissed as they carted the headboard of the bed up to the room they were to share.

"We have to set up this silly bed first. He can't have gone far. They don't move fast, do they?"

Laurel had no idea. She hoped not. She was afraid she was wrong.

At last, the bed was put together. Dad came up to help.

The girls did not draw an easy breath until he was gone. They flung sheets and blankets on. Neither of them had ever made a bed from scratch so speedily and inefficiently.

"Now," Laurel said and the search began anew.

It was Elspeth who opened the door to the room which had belonged to James and was now Lindsay's.

Lindsay was lying on the bed. Nobody had remembered her for a long time but she had not minded. Curled up beside her was a small sleepy hamster.

"How . . . how did you get him?" Laurel spluttered, running to his rescue. She halted as Lindsay clutched at him indignantly.

"Be careful," a voice said inside the older sister, experienced in the ways of four-year-olds. "She'll yell and bring Aunt Jessica."

"He's mine," Lindsay said. "I found him all by myself. He was hiding under James's dresser."

Laurel explained about Puff's escape. As she did, she realized that they were all in this together. With three of them wanting him, Aunt Jessica wouldn't stand a chance.

"I'll share him with you and Elspeth," she said hurriedly, "but don't tell. And we have to find him a box which will keep him in."

Elspeth produced a shoe box which was still intact, dumping out a pair of shoes to do it. Laurel went to the bathroom and came back with a wad of cotton wool which would make him a bed. They put him in and leaned over to look at him, their three faces wearing the same look of loving anxiety and curiosity, their three heads so different — Laurel's smooth black hair falling forward over her cheeks, Lindsay's springy curls like chicken feathers, and Elspeth's soft brown hair piled high.

At supper the three girls were unusually silent. At first, Jessica Marlowe imagined it was because they were especially hungry but not one of them had finished the first course when it was time for dessert. Lindsay was frankly dreaming about something, her blue eyes wide and happy, her mouth turning up in a private smile for which neither her aunt nor her father could determine a cause. The older girls kept their eyes down except to flash Lindsay a look of warning every so often.

James finally brought it out in the open. He had been watching Laurel as steadily as a small dog watches its master, but Laurel was too busy to notice. Something had taken her thoughts away from him. She was strangely changed, as she had been in the hall earlier.

"Laurie, you have a secret," he announced all at once, coming perilously close to the truth.

All three girls started and then stared at him. Laurel was the one who answered.

"Who says so?" she shot back at him. Her black eyebrows came together fiercely and she glared. "Quiet!" her look said.

James hushed.

"What's this?" Dad asked.

"A secret?" Aunt Jessica invited.

But now all four children were armed against the adults. James sat silent. Laurel would tell him later. He knew on which side he belonged.

"James is just making things up," Elspeth said lightly.

"You'd think we had a lion hidden in the closet or something."

At that, Lindsay gave way to a storm of giggles. Laurel glared at her small sister now but she had never been able to handle Lindsay. In a moment, the little girl was hiccoughing. Tears began to run down over her round cheeks.

"A lion," she gasped, unable to control herself. "James thinks we have a lion."

Aunt Jessica picked Lindsay up, took her to the kitchen, wiped away her tears, gave her a drink for her hiccoughs and generally returned her to herself. The other three sat at the table in anguish until Lindsay was placed in her chair again.

"Had she told?" their eyes demanded.

Lindsay caught the question and did her best with it. "I didn't say anything," she informed them. "I kept the secret. Aunt Jessica didn't even ask me."

The girls groaned, though not aloud. Their faces were bland now, unknowing. Even James, who had yet to learn what secret he was keeping, did his best to look as though he did not understand a word Lindsay said. Their blank faces were too much for Lindsay. She thought something had gone terribly wrong. Perhaps Puff had gone! Perhaps she had only imagined him.

"You know what I mean," she appealed to Laurel. "I didn't tell about the little monster. I didn't even say his name. Is he still upstairs?" she finished anxiously.

Aunt Jessica knew sense from nonsense. "Monster indeed," she said. "Hurry up, Lindsay, and eat your pudding."

"We do so have a monster," Lindsay defended herself hotly. "He's little and yellow and he's in a box in my closet right this minute and his name is Puff, so there. Isn't that right, Laurel?"

Aunt Jessica looked around at Laurel's and Elspeth's angry faces, at James's eager interest.

"Show me," Aunt Jessica said grimly.

7

Help Unwanted

Dad did not stay to meet "the monster."

"Good luck, Jessica. Don't forget your gun," he said — and left for the hospital.

The four children followed in an anxious cavalcade as Aunt Jessica marched up the stairs and into Lindsay's room. It was dark and Puff, who did his real living by night, was wide awake and scratching at the side of the box with his tiny feet. The sound was eerie and Lindsay pushed close to Laurel in the moment before their aunt found the switch and flicked on the overhead light.

"Why, you have a hamster," Aunt Jessica said. She did not sound too surprised. She did not sound too disturbed either. She went on, "What's more, you have a hungry hamster. James, run down and bring up a bit of bread and that piece of apple left over from the salad. It's still on the counter by the sink. And maybe a leaf of lettuce."

James stood and gaped at her.

"I'll go," Laurel offered at once, covering up for him as smoothly as she could. James would never manage to keep so many instructions straight. Aunt Jessica frowned at the bewilderment on her nephew's face but she made no comment as Laurel ran for the food.

I must be imagining things, Laurel thought as she located the slice of apple and went to the refrigerator for lettuce. She couldn't be — pleased!

As she started back up the stairs, it came to her that Aunt Jessica might be relieved. Maybe she had thought they had a stray dog hidden away — or even a real "monster" as Lindsay had suggested. Laurel laughed at the idea of Aunt Jessica believing, even for an instant, in monsters.

Sitting on the edge of Lindsay's bed and watching Puff have his first meal in his new home was something each of the children remembered long afterwards. He sat up on his haunches and took the bread so tidily between his small front feet. Nibble! Nibble! The bread was gone. And he was on his hind legs looking for more.

"They're so dainty," Aunt Jessica said gently. She sounded most unlike her usual busy, brisk self. She held out a bit of apple to the hamster who accepted it graciously.

"When I was a little girl, I had a white mouse," she went on dreamily. The children sat like statues. "He used to run up my sleeve and climb into my pocket sometimes. I kept any special little treat I had for him in there and he knew it."

"What was his name?" Laurel asked. She spoke softly so as not to break the spell.

"Tom Thumb. I loved all Beatrix Potter's books. I begged for a hedgehog — I planned to call her Mrs. Tiggy-winkle, of course — but nobody took me seriously. I could have had a rabbit. A boy offered me one and I was in seventh heaven but my parents said 'Nonsense' and the boy gave her to some other child. Your grandfather did not even approve of Tom Thumb. Finally, one day while I was at school, he let him out of his cage."

The children gasped. Their grandfather Demming had died before they were born but they had often heard Gran tell what a fine person he was. Now he sounded like an ogre.

"Oh, your mother drove him to it," Aunt Jessica said to the Rosses. She laughed at their horrified expressions and explained, "Susan hated Tom. We had to share a room and she was afraid of him. She was sure he'd get loose and come into bed with us some night and she said his cage smelled. I guess it did too. I know I didn't clean it as often as I should have. She nagged and nagged about him — and she was always Father's favorite, being the baby. So, one afternoon, when I came in and went to say 'Hello' to him, Tom Thumb had disappeared."

Laurel was feeding Puff the rest of the apple. Wonderful as he was, minute and delicate and delightful though she saw him to be, she now had half her mind on the small girl who had once been Jessica Demming and on her nagging younger sister Susan who was now Mama.

"What did you do?" she wanted to know.

"Was Mama glad?" Lindsay asked, unable to believe such a story about her mother.

"I want to see the mouse," James put in unexpectedly.

Laurel hushed him. "The mouse is dead. Just listen, James."

"I hunted for him but when we couldn't find any trace of him, I cried and cried. The funny thing was, Susan cried every bit as hard as I did. Father did not know what to make of her at all. When we both said we wouldn't go to bed until he was found, Father told us he had given him away — what did you say this hamster's name is?"

"Puff," Laurel said firmly.

"You'll have to get him a proper cage and some hamster food," Aunt Jessica said without batting an eyelash. "I think he's safe enough there for the night but he'd soon chew his way out if we left him there for long. Besides, he should have a treadmill and you need a cage you can keep clean."

Laurel wanted to fling her arms around Aunt Jessica's neck and hug her until it hurt but, with Elspeth sitting there watching, she couldn't. Aunt Jessica did not seem to expect any thanks. She got to her feet.

"You girls can get started on those dishes," she ordered, "and I'll get these two ready for bed."

Something inside Laurel stiffened. Aunt Jessica was interfering again. Both James and Lindsay looked uneasy. They were going to have to sleep in strange rooms and in beds which were not their own. They needed Laurel to help them get used to the new way things were.

"I'll put them to bed," Laurel said, standing up to face her aunt.

Aunt Jessica either did not hear or chose to ignore the note of challenge in Laurel's words.

"Haven't you homework to do?" she asked mildly. "I don't imagine you got much done last night."

It was useless to lie.

"But . . . but . . ." Laurel searched for a telling argument. "You said 'dishes,' not 'homework.'"

Jessica Marlowe smiled down at her. "Skip the dishes this time and concentrate on the homework," she said. "And don't worry about these two. I'll take good care of them. You need a rest from being a mother."

Laurel did not understand. She followed the others out into the room she and Elspeth were to share. Resentment was boiling up inside of her and with it, a nameless fear. What was Aunt Jessica trying to do? James and Lindsay needed her, their sister. James especially needed her. He sent her a frightened look as Aunt Jessica led him away.

"No dishes!" Elspeth chortled. "And I don't have homework yet. I guess I'd better find out where your class is in school though. I'm probably ahead. 'Briarhill has higher standards than a public school,' " she quoted with a trace of smugness.

Laurel rounded on her. No longer were they two girls sharing a secret. Elspeth was an interloper like her mother. They were invading Laurel's home. Although she herself had invited them and although she stood no chance of winning with Aunt Jessica against her, Laurel prepared to fight.

"You're crazy," she told her cousin flatly. All the pent-up feelings pounding within her made her voice savage. "And Briarhill is a crazy school. I'll bet you're miles behind us."

Elspeth backed up and sat down heavily on the edge of her bed. The lively interest which had lit her face went out as abruptly as a snuffed candle flame.

"I am not crazy," she said halfheartedly. She added, with more spirit, "Speaking of being crazy, what's come over you all at once?"

"Nothing's come over me," Laurel retorted furiously, knowing she was being unreasonable. "And I just bet you *are* behind me in school."

She reached for her science text to settle the question. Then she stopped with her hand still in mid-air. In the bathroom, behind the closed door, James and Lindsay were laughing merrily. Laurel stood as though she were frozen and listened.

"Do it again, Aunt Jessica," James shouted enthusiastically.

Aunt Jessica must have repeated her performance for the shrieks of laughter grew louder and came even more clearly to the ears of the two girls together in the bedroom next door.

Elspeth, studying Laurel's stricken face, began to understand what had made her cousin turn on her so angrily.

"Mother's probably juggling for them," she explained in a small voice. "Children always love it. She's not really good at it but they like it best of all when she drops the things."

"I don't care if she's standing on her head," Laurel responded, but she turned so that Elspeth would not be able to see the tears stinging her eyes.

This is what I wanted, the sensible Laurel told the hurt one. I called her myself. I wanted her help.

But the Laurel who flinched at each new burst of hilarity was too lonely to listen to such unwelcome truth.

I don't want her help, she insisted stubbornly, turning her back on reason. I don't need her. I wish I'd never phoned her.

"Are you two girls busy at your homework?" Aunt Jessica called a few minutes later.

Laurel had drifted back into Lindsay's room. She was sitting on the bed cradling Puff in her cupped hands and feeling sorry for herself. Elspeth had not moved. She was staring blankly at the rug between the two beds and wondering why her mother had made her come and whether there was still a chance of her being sent back to Briarhill.

At the word "homework," Laurel deposited Puff in his box and raced on tiptoe for her desk. Elspeth collided with her as she too dove in search of books.

"Yes, Mother," Elspeth called the instant she had a volume open before her.

"Stupid, it's upside down," Laurel choked.

They began to laugh then. Trying to laugh silently made it worse. Soon they were bent double, gasping with giggles, just as Lindsay had been at the table.

They were scarcely sober when Lindsay herself, dressed in a nightgown which came down to her toes, opened the door and started through the girls' room on her way to bed. She was positively shining from the bath Aunt Jessica had given her, but there was no sign of her earlier gaiety. Her head was down, her feet dragging.

"Lindsay . . ." Laurel said uncertainly when the little girl did not speak.

Lindsay looked up briefly. Her head dropped again right away but Laurel had seen the misery in her blue eyes.

"Laurie, I want Mama," she whimpered.

Then she dashed across and flung herself into Laurel's arms. Laurel held her awkwardly. With bruising clarity, she remembered Lindsay saying these very words the night before — and how it had ended. This time Laurel must help, not hurt.

I knew she needed me, a voice inside her said triumphantly.

Yet, for a long moment, Laurel simply sat and held the smaller girl, who by now was shaking with sobs, and felt helpless. Realization that Aunt Jessica would be back at any minute to make sure Lindsay was safely tucked in, jogged Laurel's mind. She had an inspiration.

"Lindsay, I heard Daddy come in a few minutes ago," she said, her voice coaxing and tender. "Why don't you go down and say 'Good-night' to him?"

Lindsay straightened and brightened. Every night, when Mama was home, she sent Lindsay to say good-night to her father.

Dad did not even try to pretend that Lindsay was not his favorite child. Laurel had always known that her father delighted especially in "Linnet," as he often called her. It made sense because, as Laurel herself saw, Lindsay was Mama all over again in miniature. Dad had time for Lindsay when he would have been too busy to bother with her or with James. The two older children were sure of his love for them. But they both knew that if they wanted Popsicles or a dime or anything else for that matter, it was the better part of wisdom to send Lindsay to do the asking.

"Daddy!" Lindsay shrilled, and she was gone.

Dad came up with her riding on his shoulder. She had brought him to see her new room and "Laurel's monster."

"Not 'monster' — hamster," Dad told her.

"He's right in my room in a box," Lindsay bragged loudly, not attempting the word "hamster."

"She's afraid of him," Elspeth told Laurel in a low voice.

Laurel did not understand at first. Was Elspeth suggesting that Lindsay was frightened of their father? Then she knew that her cousin was talking of Puff and she was right. Lindsay's little squeal as Dad leaned closer to see Puff was not joyous but scared.

Laurel joined them and saw the hamster with Lindsay's eyes. He was no longer a small, sleepy ball of golden fur. He was doing his best to climb the straight sides of the box. Scrabble, scrabble went his tiny paws. His beady eyes looked unseeingly at them. Laurel picked up the shoe box and started for the door.

"I'm taking Puff into my room," she said.

"Fly like a bird," Dad ordered Lindsay and he dumped her from high on his shoulder right into the center of the bed. This time, Lindsay's shriek was of pure delight.

"Again," she begged.

Dad rubbed his shoulder, made a long sad face, complained that she was a giant and that he was much too old and feeble. Then, as usual, he did it again.

"Leave the door halfway open," Lindsay called after him anxiously.

He did as he was bid. Then he paused and smiled at the two older girls.

Now, Laurel thought. Now is the time to tell him. James needs me to tell him.

"Dad," she said, her voice jerking unsteadily, "did you know that James still wets the bed?"

8

No, He's Not All Right!

"James what?" Dad said.

Laurel did not want to say it again, not with Elspeth listening. But there was no other way. She repeated the bald statement.

"But he's seven years old! Your mother didn't say anything about . . ."

Laurel stuck to her guns.

"He doesn't do it every night, just once in a while . . . maybe once a week," she added, wanting the facts straight. "I always get up with him and change his bed . . . but now, he's sleeping with you and I didn't know whether you knew . . ."

Mama had never mentioned this problem except when she and Laurel were alone. Laurel had always thought of it as a private burden she and her mother conspired to carry together. Somehow Mama had made it clear that this was not a trouble to be talked about with anyone else. But now, Mama was not here and Laurel could not manage by herself.

"Glory be!" Dad said.

He scratched his head. Then he sent an embarrassed look in Elspeth's direction.

"Perhaps this is something we need not mention to Jessica," he said. "Perhaps, if the need arises, you and I could deal with things somehow . . ."

Laurel was tempted, but only for an instant. It would be wonderful to have a secret with Dad, to cope together behind Aunt Jessica's back. In actual fact, it would be impossible. Laurel knew she could not hide soiled sheets and pajamas from another woman. A man might not notice things soaking in the tub. Clearly, Dad had paid no attention in the past. But Aunt Jessica would know the first time it happened. Even if Laurel took them to the laundry tubs in the basement, she could never get them washed, dried and back in the linen closet without her aunt's knowledge.

"She'll know," she told her father. Grudgingly, she added, "We'll need her help."

"Maybe you're exaggerating. He's nearly eight," Dad began hopefully.

Elspeth had not said a word. Now she interrupted with a low warning.

"Here comes Mother now."

"James wants to say 'Good-night' to Laurel," Aunt Jessica announced from the doorway. She caught sight of their guilty faces then.

"What's going on in here?" she asked. She smiled and tried to speak lightly, but her words had an edge.

"Laurel, run down and say good-night to James," Dad said hastily. But Aunt Jessica was watching him. Nobody brushed aside a question put by Jessica Marlowe. "We'll continue this discussion in the living room when you're free. Laurel has just informed me that we have a small problem, Jessica," he finished, a bit pompously.

Laurel rose to go to her brother. She stopped short at Aunt Jessica's reply.

"If you mean James, I could have told you something was wrong two years ago," she said crisply. "And I doubt that it's such a 'small' problem, John. Run along, Laurel. He's waiting."

Laurel ran. It was almost as though she were fleeing, trying to escape the hard truth in her aunt's blunt words. Suddenly, James seemed so little and off-guard alone in the big bed downstairs. He reminded her of a rabbit, a small wild rabbit whose trust she had won, and yet who was now hopping forward into a snare that she had somehow helped to set. She had not meant to harm him, she told herself miserably.

She reached the door of her parents' bedroom and saw him, his hair damp and spiky from his bath, his cheeks scrubbed till they were pink, his brown eyes behind their glasses, wide and wary, his whole self almost lost in the great expanse of the double bed. She had to swallow hard before she spoke to him.

But she did not let him see her swallow. Laurel had learned a lot in the years she had cared for James. She knew that his happiness depended on hers. If she could make him believe she was calm and cheerful, he would be too. If he glimpsed her loneliness and confusion, he too would feel alone and uncertain.

"You look like a grown-up man in Daddy's bed," she told him. "Did Aunt Jessica read you a story?"

"Yes," James's voice still shook. "She read 'The Fierce, Bad Rabbit.'"

Oh, Aunt Jessica! Laurel groaned. Lindsay loved the story of the fierce, bad rabbit who misbehaved until a hunter came and shot off his whiskers and his cotton tail. James was always upset by it. He could never understand that it was only a story. Perhaps she could make him think of something else. James, at least, was not wanting Mama.

"I'll tell you a story about a hamster named Puff," Laurel sat down on the edge of the bed and took his thin hand in her two. "Puff was only about an inch and a half long when he was born and he had no fur at all. He knew he wasn't pretty and he wondered if he would find a happy home when he grew up."

Laurel hurried to the part where Puff became covered with golden fur. She told about the day his brothers and sisters all went to happy homes and only Puff was left. Then, before James could do more than tighten his grip on her hand, she was telling about a girl named Laurel Ross coming and loving him and carrying him home inside her coat.

"Oh, that was what made you so bunchy!" James cried, but he yawned in the middle and Laurel softened her voice.

She told about hiding Puff, about his escape, about Lindsay finding him, about his new home, about clever James who guessed they had a secret . . .

But, before she was finished, his hand had grown limp and she laid it down gently. She tiptoed out of the room.

"Please, God," she prayed as she approached the living room, "don't let him wet his bed tonight."

Dad, Aunt Jessica and Elspeth were all there. They were just sitting, not saying a word.

"We had to wait for you, Laurel," Aunt Jessica said tartly, "because you appear to be the only one to know anything about your brother."

Dad looked uncomfortable. Laurel was sorry for him but queerly proud too that these adults should have to turn to her for information.

"What do you want to know?" she asked.

"James is really all right, isn't he, Laurie?" Dad said feebly. He was pleading with her and for a moment Laurel thought of closing the ranks and shutting these others out. After all, James was a Ross and theirs. Aunt Jessica had no business . . . Then the real Laurel, the girl who had lain awake nights wishing that somehow, someday, she could make somebody understand that James needed special help, won.

"No, he's not all right," Laurel said clearly. "I don't know what's wrong with him but he still isn't learning anything in school and he can't even dress himself," she finished. "I have to do it for him every morning."

9

Lindsay's Sister

Aunt Jessica nodded as though she had already guessed that much. (Of course she would, Laurel thought, she helped him get ready for bed.) Dad appeared appalled. Elspeth kept her face carefully blank. Their silence encouraged Laurel. Now that she had started to talk, now that people were actually listening to what had worried her for so long, the whole story came spilling out.

He probably could learn to dress himself but he was so slow and she had both of them to get ready, she defended herself. She told of her efforts to help him with schoolwork and her failure.

"The other kids call him Dumbo," she said. "He doesn't have any friends."

"That could be because he's too dependent on you," Aunt Jessica commented, half to herself.

Laurel plunged on. She told about the day Mama had fractured her hip, about James lying in the snow. The bruise on his face was still there.

"One time, he asked me what 'Dumbo' meant," she said.

James had asked her on the way home from school. He had thought the jeering word was spoken in friendly teasing until he had called another boy "Dumbo." The boy had threatened to punch him one. Laurel had arrived just in time.

"What does it mean, Laurie?" he had said.

Worried sick over him and furious at him for causing her such anguish, Laurel had spoken cruelly.

"It means you're dumb, stupid, a nut," she had said, each word coming at him with the sting of a slap.

"I'm not stupid," James had stuck up for himself.

"You are so!" she had hurled right back at him.

"I am not," he had repeated, but this time his defense lacked conviction. His voice had dulled.

Too late, Laurel had been sorry. Something in his face had told her that this was something he would not forget, a hurt which she had helped to give to him.

"I told him what it meant," she confessed miserably now.

After an instant of silence, she raised her head and looked at them. To her surprise, there was no blame in their eyes. If they were blaming anyone, they were blaming themselves.

"Susan must have realized . . ." Aunt Jessica said, at last, slowly.

Laurel sprang to her mother's defense.

"I look after James. Mama doesn't know he doesn't dress himself. She knows he wets the bed, but lots of kids wet their beds sometimes. Lots."

"I wet mine once when I was ten," Elspeth said.

Laurel had almost forgotten Elspeth was there. Now, she sent her a look of love.

"No one of these things would be cause for alarm in itself," Aunt Jessica said, "but what Laurel has told us adds up to quite a picture. He bites his nails badly too. I noticed them tonight when I was bathing him. He's taken them off right down to the quick."

"I bite my nails sometimes," Laurel said hotly.

But they were closing her out now. They were adults, facing an adult problem, and they were trying to think of the best way to proceed. At that moment, neither of them fully realized how long Laurel had recognized and struggled with this burden, before they had admitted its existence.

"He's your son," Aunt Jessica said. "But, if I were you, I'd ask your doctor to have him tested at the Mental Health Clinic."

"I'll make an appointment on Monday," Dad sounded tired. "I don't know what Susan will say," he added.

"I'll talk to Susan," Aunt Jessica promised. He looked at her sharply and she added, "Don't be silly, John, I'm not going to lecture her."

Laurel, knowing Aunt Jessica, was not too sure.

That night, once again, Laurel could not get to sleep. She turned the pillow over, searching for a cool place. She twisted and tossed, trying to get comfortable. She kicked off an extra blanket and fifteen minutes later got up and put it back.

"Go to sleep," she ordered herself. "Go to sleep."

But the command, which had worked for her on other nights, had no effect on her at all. Neither would her dream of flying come to her rescue. For one thing, she could hear Elspeth breathing in the next bed. Laurel had never before shared a room with anyone. James had been next door but she had had to listen hard to hear him at night. Elspeth was restless, even though she was sleeping. Several times she muttered to herself.

"But I don't want to go!" she said once, quite clearly.

"Elspeth?" Laurel whispered — but there was no answer.

Laurel's bed had been shifted to make room for Elspeth's. It had only been moved over a foot and a half so that it stood against the wall. But from there the window looked as though it were in the wrong place and the shadows seemed to crouch and loom. Usually Laurel told herself firmly, "That's only the desk with books piled on it," or "That's nothing but the closet door." But from this new angle, the darkness which was the desk, the gaping blackness of the closet door, could not be easily converted into familiar everyday things.

And there was James!

Laurel Ross had often lain awake worrying about James. Now everything was changed. He was going to be looked after. Dad was going to take him to a clinic and it would all be fixed. Surely there was nothing in that to keep her awake.

"He was mine," Laurel thought desolately to herself. "I took care of him and he was mine. And now, I told on him. I shouldn't have told. He can't help it. He's tall for seven. There's nothing really wrong with him. He's only a baby still."

The things her mother and father had said made sense to her now. She was afraid for James and she was terribly lonely. Her throat grew tight. Afraid that Elspeth would hear her crying, she turned and buried her face in the pillow.

All at once, a hand touched her shoulder.

Laurel spun around in the darkness, gasping with shock. In the faint light from the window, she could see Lindsay standing beside her, shivering with cold. Laurel was thankful her own face was in darkness.

"What is it?" she managed.

She whispered so as not to waken Elspeth and Lindsay answered in a whisper.

"I had a bad dream . . . a fox came and got in my bed . . . he said he'd eat me . . . he had big teeth like carving knives!"

Her voice was rising; in another instant, she would be howling with fright. Laurel reached out and put a hand over her little sister's mouth.

"Sh," she ordered sternly. She herself had completely forgotten her own fears. Her eyes were dry and her voice low and steady.

"Get in here with me. Hurry up. Oo-oo-oo, your toes are like icicles!"

Lindsay half sobbed, half giggled. She snuggled close to

her big sister. Always before, she had taken her bad dreams straight to Mama but tonight, in desperation, she had come to Laurel and Laurel was cuddling her and making her terror dissolve exactly as Mama did.

"You're just . . . like Mama," she whispered into Laurel's ear, her words broken by an enormous yawn.

Laurel smiled in the darkness. Where did Lindsay think she had learned how to comfort a little girl with a nightmare? Laurel remembered herself, at Lindsay's age, scuttling through the darkness to the haven of her mother's arms.

It was crowded but, curled up together like two spoons, neither of the girls minded. Soon they both slept.

James did not wet the bed that night.

10

Monday Morning

Sunday was a quiet day. The children took turns holding and petting Puff until he became so upset at not getting his daily sleep that he bit Elspeth's finger.

They left him alone after that, although the bite was not serious.

They went to church in the morning and Dad and Aunt Jessica went together to visit Mama during the afternoon, leaving Elspeth and Laurel in charge. Mama had made it a rule that homework be done before Sunday but Dad said that this time should be an exception. So Elspeth played with Lindsay and James while Laurel did her math.

The next morning, when Laurel was helping James on with his boots and Elspeth was waiting, Aunt Jessica changed Laurel's life once again.

"I'll finish getting him ready," she said casually. "I'm

driving him to school when I take Lindsay to the nursery school. You two girls can walk."

James was pleased this time. He loved cars.

"Br-r-rum, brr-r-rum," he said, pretending he was one.

Dazed by the suddenness of it, Laurel walked out the front door with Elspeth close behind her. She was actually walking to school with another girl her own age!

Laurel introduced Elspeth to her home-room teacher. Miss Roe smiled at Elspeth. "Your mother called about you," she said. "We were so sorry to hear about your mother's accident, Laurel. I imagine you are a little ahead of this class, Elspeth. Briarhill is noted for its high academic standards."

Elspeth blushed, said nothing and carefully did not look at Laurel. She was given the empty seat behind Laurel's. From across the aisle, Barbara West studied her. Laurel, catching the look, tried to imagine what Barbara must be thinking. Probably, "How could Laurel Ross have a glamorous cousin like that!"

Laurel bit her lip and kept her head high. Then Barbara leaned toward her and whispered, "Is he all right?"

"Who?" Laurel whispered back, her face blank.

Before Barbara said "Butterball," Laurel remembered. She glowed happily at the other girl. For a moment, the reserve between them vanished. "He's just fine," Laurel told his first owner. "He was fast asleep when I left home. He eats EVERYTHING! Only some things, he just tucks away in the corner for later."

Barbara nodded and was about to say something else when Miss Roe called the class to attention.

They had math first.

"Laurel," Elspeth hissed from behind her, "we haven't taken this yet. How do you do it?"

Laurel tried not to look smug when she turned to help but she could feel her eyes dancing. Elspeth was not embarrassed, however; she was too interested in the new problem. Laurel flipped back a page or two in the text and showed her the sample questions. In no time, Elspeth's face cleared.

"Oh, I see," she said and bent over her work.

Turning back to her own, Laurel realized, all at once, that Elspeth went at schoolwork the way she herself did. It was a challenge, a puzzle to be solved. She never admitted it out loud but she thought some subjects were fun. Laurel loved geography and history and she enjoyed mathematics. She disliked English composition because she could not seem to make a story come alive. She could tell a story but words which came easily when she spoke resisted her stiffly when she tried to put them down on paper. Barbara always got the highest marks in the class in English. When the teacher read Barbara's stories aloud, Laurel was awed by the things Barbara did with words. But it comforted her to know that Barbara was easily muddled in math and disliked science intensely. What about Elspeth? Of course, Elspeth would only be in the class for six weeks. Still, they got their reports just before Christmas. Suppose Elspeth were good at everything!

"Get to work, Laurel," Miss Roe said. She was surprised to find Laurel sitting with her pencil idle in her hand and her surprise was in her voice. Laurel flushed and began to dash down figures so speedily that she put a whole column in the wrong place and had to stop and erase. She bit her lip and began again, forcing herself to work properly, shutting Barbara and Elspeth out of her thoughts.

When the girls came out of the building at noon, Laurel looked anxiously for James. When she saw him, safe and sound on the steps, she drew a deep breath of relief. Then she saw Aunt Jessica waiting with him.

"I'm taking him home with me," she called. James waved and they disappeared into the crowd of milling children.

"Laurel, are you all right?" Elspeth asked.

"Yes, I'm fine," Laurel answered unevenly. She could not explain what had held her there, staring at the place where James had vanished. She had yearned to be free and now that freedom was hers, it seemed forced and wrong. She had hated having to drag James along wherever she went, day after day! Yet, now that Aunt Jessica had taken over the responsibility, Laurel felt robbed.

"Let's go, Laurel," Elspeth said.

As Laurel turned and met her cousin's gaze, her heart lifted for an instant.

"We're almost friends," Elspeth's smile said and Laurel's answering smile agreed. As they started home side by side, she almost forgot that James had been taken from her.

The dry snow squeaked under their boots. Although the sun shone and the sky was blue overhead, a sharp wind stung their faces. Soon Elspeth's cheeks were scarlet. Laurel, noticing, laughed.

"If only Mrs. Birch could see you now!" she exclaimed.

"Why?"

Laurel explained about Mrs. Birch and "rosy cheeks" and Elspeth grinned.

"Well, the tip of your nose is quite pink. You look like a rabbit," she said, studying Laurel's face with interest.

"It feels frozen! Let's run," Laurel shivered.

They raced off down the street. Neither of them noticed Barbara West.

She had almost caught up to them when, suddenly, unaccountably, they sped away from her. She stood still and watched them getting smaller in the distance. Then, she bent her head and trudged doggedly on.

If they did not want to walk with her, that was fine with her, she told herself.

Even if they had explained that they had not realized she was there, Barbara would not have believed them. It had taken courage to try to catch up with them. She still remembered the day Laurel had refused to walk home with her months before. She had been foolish to imagine that Laurel's taking the hamster might change all that.

She made a picture in her mind of herself marching over to Rosses and demanding that her hamster be returned. She would be very cool about it, but relentless. Even as she told herself she would do just that the moment she reached home, she knew she could not. For one thing, her mother would never permit it.

If only Laurel had taken time to tell her how he was. She had started to say something, but had not bothered to finish, although there had been plenty of time between periods.

He was fine. He was sound asleep in one corner of the cookie tin into which Aunt Jessica had moved him until they bought a proper cage. The girls leaned over the box and Laurel called his name softly.

"Puff . . . Puff . . ."

He did not stir.

"Leave him alone, Laurel," Aunt Jessica said. "You shouldn't bother him during the day."

Laurel glowered but Aunt Jessica had gone to the cupboard for the salt and pepper shakers and she did not notice.

Laurel kept sulkily silent till lunch was half over. Then she forgot about herself as Dad turned to James and said, too loudly, too cheerfully, "Son, I'm writing your teacher a note to let you out of school early. I've made an appointment for you to have a check-up."

"A check-up!" James echoed blankly.

"You remember, James," Laurel plunged in. "You had a check-up in the summer. I took you and Dr. Fullbright looked in your ears and down your throat — "

Too late she remembered how much James had hated having his throat examined. His face darkened and his lip stuck out mutinously.

"I don't want a check-up," he stated.

Dad shot a look of pure exasperation at Laurel. At the same moment, Aunt Jessica said smoothly, "Big boys have medical check-ups before they go to camp and men have them when they're going into the army. I saw you playing army yesterday, James. Did you remember that all the men had to have a check-up?"

"No — " James said. His voice wavered uncertainly.

"When you come home," Aunt Jessica said firmly, "we'll have to have a special supper for you men. The rest of us are having soup but maybe, if you've just had a check-up, you and your Dad should have cheeseburgers."

How had Aunt Jessica discovered James's devotion to cheeseburgers? Laurel saw her brother's face clear. Dad grinned at Aunt Jessica. Laurel suddenly felt she did not belong in the warm family before her. James did not need her. She was only a bother. Dad's glance had made that plain.

At that instant, Lindsay whispered, "Laurel, I'm done. May I be excused?"

Laurel stared at her. Lindsay looked solemnly back. Aunt Jessica was giving James a second helping of pudding. Dad was busy eating.

"Yes," Laurel said right out loud. Aunt Jessica looked up, startled. Dad's hand, holding a cup of coffee, halted in mid-air. Laurel had surprised herself too but she did not show it. She kept her eyes on Lindsay.

"You may be excused," she told her.

Lindsay did not slide down from her chair. She wriggled a little as though something in the atmosphere made her uncomfortable.

"May I go and look at your little lobster, if I don't wake him up?" she inquired. "I'll be still as a mouse."

"Sure," Laurel said.

Her cheeks felt hot now. She and Lindsay seemed to be talking to each other in the middle of a great pool of listening silence.

"Good coffee, Jessica," Dad said abruptly. He pushed back his chair. "I'll come to your classroom to get you, son," he told James. Lindsay slipped away. Laurel hurried to finish. What was Aunt Jessica thinking?

"How much will a cage cost?" Aunt Jessica asked.

Elspeth answered, describing two kinds of cages.

"You'd better get the more expensive one," her mother said. "It sounds like a lot but, in the long run, you get what you pay for."

Laurel gulped. That was exactly what Mama would have said. Laurel had heard her over and over again.

"No more, James," Aunt Jessica went on. "Enough is as good as a feast."

She looked up in amazement then as Laurel burst out laughing. But was she laughing? Her eyes shone with tears.

"Laurel . . ." Aunt Jessica said, "what is it?"

"You sound just like Mama, just exactly," Laurel told her. She knew it was not really funny. A moment before, she had been ready to cry about it. But now, she shook with laughter.

"Like Susan?" Aunt Jessica clearly had not the least idea how they were alike.

James and Elspeth were laughing now too. Elspeth was laughing because Laurel's explosion of giggles was catching but James had heard what Laurel had.

"You said, 'Enough is as good as a feast,'" he told her.

"And 'you get what you pay for,'" Laurel quoted, sobering a little.

Aunt Jessica laughed herself now.

"Oh, if that's all it takes," she said, "how about 'Waste not, want not' and 'In for a penny, in for a pound!' and 'Six of one and half a dozen of the other . . .' or 'Slow as molasses in January.' "

"Does Aunt Susan say all those things too?" Elspeth asked delightedly.

"Of course, she does," Aunt Jessica said. "We had the same mother, remember, and she brought us up on those. How about 'Whistling girls and crowing hens always come to bad ends.' "

The sound of their laughter, now simmering down, had drawn Lindsay back into the room. She looked at them gravely and then remarked, "I like 'So's Christmas.' "

The rest of them stared at her.

"What did you say, Lindsay?" Laurel put in at last. Lindsay remained perfectly serious.

"When Mama calls me, then I say 'I'm coming . . .' " she began to explain.

Then they all caught it.

"And she says, 'So's Christmas,' " they chorused.

This time, even Aunt Jessica laughed till the tears came.

11

Almost a Quarrel

"I was brave, Laurie," James boasted when he and Dad came in.

The girls were watching Puff make himself at home in his new cage and Elspeth and Lindsay barely glanced up. Laurel had been waiting and wondering all afternoon. She looked searchingly at her father but his face was inscrutable.

"Brave," she echoed, transferring her attention to James. "What did you have to be brave about?"

"I opened my mouth and said 'Ahh!'" James offered hopefully.

"Any baby can do that," Lindsay said in her most disagreeable voice, keeping her back turned.

"I am not a baby," James began.

"Of course, you're not — and you were brave," Laurel reassured him gently.

She would have turned on Lindsay a few days before. In those few days, however, Laurel Ross had grown in her understanding of others. She knew in herself the jealousy which twisted in her small sister. She ignored Lindsay and knelt to undo James's coat.

"Puff has a new cage, James," she told him.

"A new cage," James repeated, his face lighting with wonder and eagerness to see.

"Laurel, let him do that for himself," Aunt Jessica's voice, sharp as a knife blade, thrust between them.

Laurel looked blankly at her aunt. Then, she realized. She was waiting on James. But this was his good coat with big buttons and stiff new buttonholes all the way down the front.

"He can't . . ." she began.

Aunt Jessica did not let her finish. She came swiftly over and put her hand on James's shoulder, backing him a couple of steps away from the big sister who had always taken care of him. James now looked anything but brave.

"You *can* undo your own coat, James. I'll show you how," his aunt said firmly. "A man should be able to deal with his own buttons," she added, a little more gently.

James, fighting tears, started to fumble ineffectively with the buttons.

"No, no," Jessica Marlowe said after watching him struggle for less than a minute. She was doing her best to sound patient but both James and Laurel heard the effort it cost her to control her voice.

Laurel glimpsed the truth in that instant. Aunt Jessica was right, she thought. James must be taught, but Aunt

Jessica was wrong too because Aunt Jessica was not the person who should teach him.

Fumbling with words as awkwardly as James fumbled with buttons, Laurel tried to help.

"Let me, Aunt Jessica," she said. "I won't do it for him, I promise, but maybe, if I could show him . . . Maybe he should start with his windbreaker. It has a zipper."

Aunt Jessica missed the entreaty in Laurel's stammered offer. She heard only, "Let me, Aunt Jessica."

"James is doing fine," she silenced her niece. "Now, James, use your head. Push it through the hole; don't pull it."

Hot with resentment, hurt by the despair in James's thin face, Laurel escaped to her room. Hunched miserably, she sat on the bed and wondered what was happening.

She began to think of how she would have helped her brother had she been given the chance. Then she straightened, her face blank with astonishment.

Why, Aunt Jessica did not know how to undo buttons any more than James did! She heard, over again, her aunt's instructions. "Push it through; don't pull it." How *did* you undo a coat? Surely you didn't "push" the buttons.

Laurel stood up, went quickly to the closet and got an old housecoat of her own, one which buttoned. She put it on — not thinking through what she was doing, just experimenting for her own satisfaction — and tried buttoning and unbuttoning it. Her fingers felt stiff and unwieldy as though they were unfamiliar with buttons. At last, she had it straight. She knew how to explain it to James. If only Aunt Jessica — but Aunt Jessica had made it obvious that

help from Laurel was the last thing she needed or wanted.

Laurel sat down with a thump. She was discouraged, but she had the beginnings of an idea. It turned over in her mind and became words.

Everything should be taught to him like this, she mused. I don't know how I do things and neither does Aunt Jessica and so we can't teach James. He can't just pick things up the way we do. Somebody should do each thing, ordinary things like dressing and setting the table, until she knows just exactly how she does it. Then she could show James one step at a time . . .

"Laurel!"

Elspeth, with Puff's cage in her arms, stood in the doorway. It was a second before Laurel connected her cousin's widened eyes with the housecoat she herself had on over her school clothes.

She felt foolish for a moment. Then she forgot herself as she remembered James.

"What's happening?" she asked.

"Mother took his coat off for him," Elspeth kept her voice carefully flat. Laurel understood. After all, Aunt Jessica was Elspeth's mother. "She said she guessed he'd better begin with his other coat. But why are you wearing that?"

Laurel explained. Elspeth looked thoughtful. Then she said slowly, "Ye-e-es. When you brush your teeth, for instance . . . first you take the lid off the toothpaste and then . . . or do you get your brush out of the holder first? Does James do his own teeth?"

"He brushes them but I put the toothpaste on his brush

and get him a drink and put the lid back on . . . but to-night, I'll . . ."

"Don't teach him everything at once," Elspeth warned, wise beyond her years. "He's had enough today with that coat business. Oh, I almost forgot. Mother said to come to supper. Hurry up and get out of that thing."

When James, having brushed his teeth as usual, was in bed, Laurel went to her father to ask what Dr. Fullbright had said.

"Laurel, you shouldn't worry about him so much," Dad told her. "Your Aunt Jessica thinks you're far too old for your age. We've given you too much responsibility . . ."

He looked at her then and his words petered out. Her face was full of waiting and yet, her eyes were afraid. John Ross did not often see into his children's hearts. As he looked into Laurel's, he realized that it was too late to scold at her. She was bearing an anxiety equal to his own.

He sighed and reported that James was to be seen at the Mental Health Clinic. The earliest appointment to be had, however, was almost a month away. James had been lucky to get it. There had been a cancellation.

"Dick Fullbright says he's healthy enough physically," he went on. "His coordination isn't what it might be and, of course, he's shortsighted. But then, so are you and so am I. Dick did say though that he thought we were wise to have him seen at the Clinic. I explained all you told us and he asked me why I hadn't been in long ago. I had to tell him then that I didn't have the whole picture until you came out with it. He said you were a good girl, Laurel. He also said that we adults could learn a lesson from you.

'Facing facts' he called it. I felt about two feet high when he finished. I don't think he felt too good himself. I don't know what your mother is going to say when I tell her."

It came to Laurel, all at once, that Mama would probably be glad. Mama was a person who let things slide. She was not forever setting everyone straight as Aunt Jessica did. But all the same, Mama had known about the bed-wetting. Mama had seen James's chewed-off fingernails. Mama may not have realized exactly how helpless James was at getting dressed, but she did know that Laurel did his coat up every morning. Mama had heard Laurel trying to help James learn to read. Mama had been aware that James could not get to school alone. Even though Mama had said, over and over, "There's nothing the matter. He's only a baby," Laurel had a feeling that Mama had stopped believing in her own words. However shocked Mama was on top, underneath she would surely be relieved.

Having settled Lindsay for the night, Jessica Marlowe joined the other two in the living room. Dad told her about James's appointment in December.

"I think it is shocking that we'll have to wait a whole month before he can be seen at the Clinic," Aunt Jessica said indignantly.

Laurel did not say a word as her father explained again about the cancellation. She herself was glad that there would be another month before they would know anything more. Mama might be home by then, and James somehow would be safer with Mama home.

"Mentally retarded . . ." Laurel shied away from the words. Aunt Jessica had been the one to use them. She had said bluntly that she would be most surprised if James were not mentally retarded.

If the people at the Clinic agreed with her, if they said that James was indeed retarded, would he still be James? Laurel had a recurring, unreasoning fear that the very words would somehow change him. His mouth would hang ajar. His brown eyes would become fixed and dull. He would not laugh any longer. He would not ask for Teeny Tiny Woman stories.

Laurel shivered and ordered herself to stop being silly. How could a couple of words make James into a different boy? James was James and that was all there was to it.

But the fear persisted just the same.

That night, when the two girls were in bed with the light out, Elspeth confided, "I like school here. Everything's so different —"

Laurel was deep in thoughts of James and she only half heard. "Different," she said, repeating the one word she was sure of. "How 'different?' "

"Well, at Briarhill there are no boys for one thing," Elspeth explained. "And we all have to wear uniforms. The uniform is horrible!"

Laurel was too stunned to comment. She had envied Elspeth that trim school uniform for years. She could not believe that Elspeth really meant she disliked it.

"And coming home for lunch is different . . . and sharing a room with you . . . and having Puff," Elspeth went on dreamily. "My whole life here is different," she finished.

"*Your* whole life!" Laurel exclaimed as though Elspeth had said something ridiculous.

Elspeth was startled at Laurel's response. She was puzzled too. She waited for Laurel to go on. A minute passed with aching slowness. Laurel said no more.

"I'm sleepy," Elspeth yawned without convincing anyone. "Good night."

She turned her back on Laurel and lay wondering what she had said to bring that note into her cousin's voice.

What had Laurel said exactly? The words played back in Elspeth's mind. "*Your* whole life!"

Laurel could only have meant one thing. Somehow, Elspeth's coming had changed Laurel's life. Elspeth remembered then, with a pang, how she had hated the thought of spending six weeks in Riverside. She heard herself begging, "Mother, please let me board at Briarhill until you come back."

Laurel must have felt the same way about her coming. Things had not gone smoothly between them on earlier visits. Elspeth relived some of those days. She had felt awkward and tongue-tied amid the teasing and squabbling which were part of Ross family life. Her clothes had also set her apart. She had never had play clothes like Laurel's, clothes you could get comfortably dirty, clothes you could tear without anyone minding. James had been another problem. Laurel had been so bound up with him that they had had to take him along everywhere. Lindsay with her soft yellow curls, her blue eyes, her enchanting giggle, her pudgy clinging hands, had appealed to Elspeth. But when she had suggested that, since they were taking James, they take Lindsay too, Laurel had scowled and given in reluctantly. Then, whether they went to a movie or on a picnic or simply for a walk, the four of them had somehow split up so that it became Elspeth and Lindsay ranged against Laurel and James.

"It was Mother too," Elspeth admitted silently.

She and her mother were friends when the two of them were alone in their apartment in Toronto. But, when they visited the Rosses, Aunt Susan with her open, easy kindness, her way of giving a quick hug or kiss for no special reason, her ready laugh, her "spoiling" of the children — as her sister called it — had made Elspeth's mother seem interfering and bossy. Whenever Mother said, "Susan, why can't you keep this kitchen organized in a rational manner?" Elspeth had reddened with embarrassment. Why couldn't Mother understand that that was just the way Aunt Susan was, the way Aunt Susan was meant to be?

Laurel had minded too. Elspeth had seen Laurel's chin jut out when Aunt Susan just laughed at Mother's sharpness. "It's too late to change me now, Jess," she would say. "Console yourself with the thought that you did your best with me when I was young."

"Oh Mama!" Laurel had said once.

And Aunt Susan had sent her a laughing glance and teased, "Laurel's still working on reforming me. I may be a credit to you both yet."

No wonder Laurel minded having us come, Elspeth thought now. It did not cross Elspeth's mind that Laurel imagined her Aunt Jessica to be right, that Laurel was as dismayed by her own mother's behavior as Elspeth was by hers.

This time, everything had gone differently right from the first. Aunt Susan had not been there to be nagged. Mother had reorganized the kitchen to her heart's content. James had been moved downstairs and into a life of his own. The two of them had shared an adventure with Puff on the day she arrived. Everything had seemed so much better.

"I thought we were friends," Elspeth mourned. She looked back now with horror on the way she and her mother had bulldozed into Laurel's life, moved James, shoved Elspeth in as her roommate without even asking —

"She doesn't want me here. She never did before and she doesn't now. She's just being polite."

Elspeth faced what she thought was the truth. It was hard to accept but she forced herself to down it. She was beginning to feel noble. She would keep out of Laurel's way from now on, she determined. She could not leave without making a scene, but she would not bother her cousin any more than she absolutely had to.

Loneliness washed over her but she fought her way clear and held onto her resolve to be a martyr.

Laurel, meanwhile, had been struck dumb by sheer surprise.

Always she had thought of Elspeth as the one who had everything she wanted. Now was Elspeth trying to make her believe that coming home for lunch was, for her, a special treat? She struggled to see the world she knew through Elspeth's eyes. She, Laurel, had been so busy coping with the disconcerting changes in her own life.

Mama was gone from her. James was no longer her charge. She now shared a room with her cousin. She had acquired a hamster. She had discovered in Lindsay a little girl she had not known before. Dad had finally listened to her and something was being done about James. Everything that had seemed stable and sound had turned upside-down. She had even begun to wonder if she and Elspeth were becoming real friends. She hardly knew how to behave sometimes. Sometimes she wondered if she might be imagining it all, only she knew she couldn't be.

Now, with a jolt, she was reminded that she was not the only one adventuring in a new world. Elspeth was facing as many changes as she, perhaps even more. Could Elspeth, too, be feeling confused and dismayed by it all?

She looked at the facts and admitted that Elspeth had good reason for feeling uprooted and cast adrift. Why, she had had to leave all her friends and come to Riverside with only twenty-four hours' notice! Elspeth must hate going to a public school after Briarhill. Who wouldn't hate it? What had Elspeth said — something about "boys."

Laurel, who seldom spoke to the boys in her class, shivered with sympathy for Elspeth. Now it was she who twisted her cousin's words until they were unrecognizable. She understood the things Elspeth had been too tactful to say. Elspeth, with a room of her own which had been specially decorated for her, felt crowded and unhappy in this room she must share with Laurel. Laurel wrinkled up her nose at the odds and ends of furniture which filled the room. Nothing matched, nothing at all. Elspeth missed her friends at Briarhill, those girls always mentioned in Aunt Jessica's letters — Maureen, Sally, Joanne. Elspeth missed eating in the big school dining room with its buzz of talk. Elspeth had spoken of Puff, but Laurel knew that at Briarhill Elspeth rode a horse. What was a scrap of a hamster compared to the glory of a horse?

"Elspeth," Laurel ventured at last into the stillness. Her voice groped uncertainly. Maybe Elspeth would speak a comforting word. Everything had seemed so much happier this time. Maybe Elspeth had felt it too.

But Laurel had waited too long. Elspeth, also wounded and unsure, was silent now. What to Laurel had seemed only a few seconds of pondering, to Elspeth had seemed an eternity. Laurel listened. Perhaps Elspeth had fallen asleep. She was breathing evenly, but each breath quivered. Laurel, who had listened to James so often, knew that her cousin was only pretending.

She doesn't want to have to talk to me, Laurel thought wretchedly. She did not speak again.

After half an hour had passed without sleep coming, Laurel made one attempt to escape into the old dream of flying. But the inner world of sun and wind into which she had soared so thankfully in the past was no longer real to her. She tried hard. She pictured the countryside below, dotted with toy trees and houses, patchworked with fields. It was like a child's drawing. To the child she had been, it had held meaning. But sometime in the last day or two she had stopped being that child. It seemed artificial and silly.

Laurel cried then.

In the morning, Aunt Jessica took James to school again. Laurel, who had been dazed by freedom the day before, now trudged along in silence. Elspeth was just as ill at ease.

Laurel saw Barbara West walking ahead of them on the other side of the street.

"Barbara," she called, breaking into a run, "wait."

"There's Barbara," she flung over her shoulder, unnecessarily, at her cousin.

Elspeth hurried after her thankfully. The three girls came together at the corner.

"Now she won't have to be alone with me," Laurel thought.

But Barbara was as distant as the other two. They made difficult, polite conversation for the last two blocks. Each of them was sure that she was the one the other two resented.

That morning Miss Roe told them about the class play.

12

Marguerite

The play was called "The Secret Gift," she told them. It was a story about a family with five children. The two oldest, Nicholas and Marguerite, had the main parts. Miss Roe went on to explain the plot. The father of the family had gone bankrupt, through no fault of his own, and he had had to tell the children that there would be no Christmas presents. Then Nicholas and Marguerite got the younger children together and made a plan somehow to buy a gift for their parents who had always given them so much. The present and the plan for getting it were to be kept secret. The children came up with several schemes, each more ridiculous than the last. But, in the end, they managed to surprise everyone, themselves included, with the present they purchased.

The plot reminded Laurel of *The Story of the Treasure Seekers*. She loved E. Nesbit and she listened eagerly. She had never had a part in a play. She had been an angel in the church pageant once but that was a different thing altogether. All she had had to do was stand and look solemn and move just enough to make her wings shimmer. There had been several school plays but she had been too shy to try for a part. And for a long time now, there had been James.

"Would those interested in taking part please raise their hands," Miss Roe said. "Don't forget it will mean staying in after four to practice."

The teacher's last words reached out to Laurel. She could do it! She could stay after four if she liked. She was free to choose. Elspeth had had a good part in a play at Briarhill the year before.

Miss Roe was reading out the names as she wrote them down.

"Rosemary Markham . . . Herb Schmidt . . . Bob Travers . . . Laurel Ross . . ."

Laurel pulled her hand down. She had done it. She swallowed and tried to pay attention. Barbara's name was called. Sam Jones . . . Maggie de Vries . . . Brian Little . . .

Miss Roe stopped. Laurel turned her head and looked at her cousin. Elspeth was just sitting, her hands folded on her desk lid. Elspeth was not even going to try for a part.

Laurel opened her mouth to ask why, but then she remembered. Elspeth could do what she liked. Laurel straightened around in her seat and faced front. She stared unseeing at the chalkboard. She could not understand why she felt so alone. After all, Elspeth had come to Riverside only three days ago. A three-day-old friendship could not matter much.

Elspeth's sense of aloneness was almost identical. Elspeth too had trouble explaining it to herself.

At four o'clock, Elspeth left the classroom. Laurel, staying to audition, told herself that her cousin was relieved to get away. Elspeth, walking by herself along the windy street, wished that Laurel had asked her to wait.

"Your turn, Laurel," Miss Roe said.

Laurel had to read a speech of Marguerite's. Marguerite was lonely and discouraged. She had tried so hard to earn money but she had only led her brothers and sisters into trouble. Now, it was Christmas Eve and they had no present at all.

Laurel had been sitting, waiting for her turn. To keep from thinking of Elspeth going off without her, she had read the one speech over and over, her head bent low over the book. When the teacher called her name, she knew the words almost by heart. What was more, she knew how Marguerite was feeling — a little desperate, unable to understand where she had gone wrong, and terribly alone.

All of this was in Laurel Ross's voice as she read. When she finished and looked up, her throat aching, her face dazed, there was a quick spatter of applause from the other boys and girls.

"I don't think that leaves much doubt about who should play Marguerite," Miss Roe smiled.

Laurel stared at her, dumbfounded. She had not once thought of being given the leading role. She had never been good at making speeches. She told stories, but only to James and sometimes Lindsay. She was nervous in front of a strange audience.

Miss Roe did not seem to notice her silence. She went on to assign the rest of the parts. When she came to Barbara, she said:

"Barbara, I wonder if you could understudy the part of Marguerite. We haven't had understudies in other years but right now, with so much flu in town, I hate to take a chance. We need someone who could step in and do a good job if anything happened to Laurel."

Barbara nodded. Laurel, who had been feeling a little like Alice falling headlong down the rabbit hole, regained her balance at the sight of Barbara's face. Laurel knew, even if Miss Roe did not, that the only reason Barbara was nodding was that she could not trust herself to speak. Barbara minded, really minded deep inside. Laurel thought back to the playlet they had done last spring about the founding of Riverside. Barbara had not had the lead but she had been good. It had been surprising how good she was, how the shy quiet Barbara had disappeared and a twinkling, witty Barbara had come to take her place. How awful to be asked to understudy!

Yet, Laurel reasoned, as they gathered their books, Miss Roe was right. Nearly a third of the class had been missing from school that day.

Barbara dove into her locker.

"I have to hurry," she said, her voice muffled.

"Well, so do I," countered Laurel.

She was into her coat as speedily as Barbara. They went

out of the building side by side, without looking at each other.

"Why do you have to care so much?" Laurel thought rebelliously. "I didn't ask to be Marguerite."

They were in front of Barbara's house before they knew it. Barbara stopped in her tracks then, faced Laurel in the November darkness and blurted, "I'm glad you're going to be Marguerite. You're just right for it."

She bolted then. Laurel stood still staring after her for a minute, but the wind worried at her till she moved on again.

When they were all at the supper table that night, she told them about her part. Dad beamed at her. Aunt Jessica said, "That's the kind of thing she's been needing, John." And Laurel looked away from the guilt in her father's eyes. Elspeth struggled with words, but finally she said gruffly, "I'm glad."

Laurel thought of telling them about Barbara. She did say, "Barbara West is my understudy," and Elspeth's eyes widened. The others were no longer listening. James had taken much too much ketchup.

That evening, when the two older girls were supposed to be deep in homework, Lindsay crept out of bed and slipped in to join them, keeping a weather eye on the door for fear of Aunt Jessica. Laurel knew she should take her right back and Elspeth knew it too, but the silence between them had grown so large and difficult that they were both delighted when Lindsay rescued them from themselves.

"I'll tell you a story, girls," she said, perching on Laurel's bed. "Are you listening?"

They assured her they were.

"One day, Mama went to the top of a high, high mountain," she said dreamily. The other girls let their pencils idle. They both loved to hear Lindsay telling a story in the small special voice she used only for "making up things."

"When she stood on the top, she said to herself, 'Oh my goodness gracious, I must be at the top of the sky.' Then she came running down with steps as big as a giant's and she jumped over oceans and parks and houses and everything — and she came home to me."

There was a lump in Laurel's throat as Lindsay finished. The little girl's face was so round and clean and sweet — and her eyes were so wistful.

"I'll tell you one now," Laurel said impulsively, going to sit beside her on the bed.

" 'The Little Red Hen,' " Lindsay said at once, "and I'll be all the animals."

The wistfulness was gone. Lindsay had clearly planned the whole thing. Or had she? Laurel gaped at her. Elspeth laughed out loud.

"Okay," Laurel said slowly. Then she too laughed and started, "Once upon a time . . ."

The warmth of that half hour stayed with them for the rest of the evening. After Lindsay had said, "Then I'll eat it myself!" and been sent to bed, Laurel almost risked asking Elspeth why she had not tried out for a play part. But she was wary of breaking the friendliness which now held them. She picked up her pencil and went back to her math. Elspeth did not ask for any help that night.

13

You're Not Going to Quit!

"**D**on't talk so loudly, Nick. Mother will be sure to hear you," Rosemary Markham, who was playing Marigold, half whispered the words.

There was an expectant silence. Laurel looked at Herb Schmidt. He looked right back at her.

"Be quiet yourself, Marigold . . ." Miss Roe prompted patiently.

"What's the matter with you, Laurel," Herb hissed as Laurel still stood waiting for someone to speak. "That's *your* line, you dope."

Laurel gasped, searched for the words she had just heard, lost them . . . Then she heard them repeated near her, so softly that the sound reached no one else.

"Be quiet yourself, Marigold," she said crossly to Rosemary. "You're the one who screamed yesterday when Father opened the door before Nick could hide the scarf."

"That's better, Laurel," Miss Roe interrupted. "You're beginning to put some feeling in your speeches. That sounded just like an older sister. All right, Herb, go ahead. 'I'd tell you, if you'd both listen for one moment . . .' "

Herb went on. Herb never made a mistake, never missed a line. Already, without costumes or scenery, he could make Laurel see another boy standing there, a boy called Nicholas. Nicholas stood straighter than Herb. Nicholas had an old-fashioned turn of phrase. Even Nicholas's voice was different, lighter somehow with a trace of an English accent.

But she, Laurel, was never going to be able to make Marguerite come alive. Everybody knew it by now, even Miss Roe, even Laurel herself.

"Laurel, when the others are talking, you have to listen," Miss Roe interrupted again. "You have to *be* Marguerite every moment you are on stage, not just when you are making a speech. That goes for the rest of you too," she added, including the others in the cast with a wave of her hand.

They all knew though that Laurel was the one she meant most. At last the rehearsal was over. It seemed to Laurel that she was the only one who stumbled over her lines, the only one who came in too quickly, the only one who forgot to face the audience, the only one who mumbled.

"I'm glad Elspeth isn't here to see," she thought as she went for her coat.

Elspeth would be there though. The whole family would

be there, even Lindsay. They had promised to come on the night she proudly told them she was to be the leading lady. Dad had taken out his appointment book and jotted it down while she watched.

She and Barbara walked halfway home in silence. Then Laurel swallowed and made herself speak.

"Thanks for telling me my lines," she muttered.

Barbara had been so close to her, sitting right there in the front desk. Miss Roe, standing at the back of the room so that the actors would have to speak out, did not guess how often Barbara had prompted Laurel.

"Oh, that's okay," Barbara returned. They walked another block in silence. Then, Barbara took a deep breath and offered, "You were fine that first day. You'll be fine again once you get over your stage fright."

"I won't," Laurel exploded. Her voice was shaking and she fought to steady it. "I just can't do it and you know it. Everybody knows it. You'd be much better than me. I'm going to tell Miss Roe so tomorrow."

They had halted and now stood facing each other in the middle of the snowy sidewalk.

"But . . . but . . ." Barbara began feebly.

Laurel stormed on, burning her bridges behind her.

"I can't 'put feeling in.' I just plain don't know how. And when she says 'Face the audience,' and I look out and see those rows and rows of desks, I get so rattled I can't think straight, let alone 'be' Marguerite. And I just don't *have* a loud voice and . . ."

"It's loud enough right now," Barbara said dryly.

Laurel stared at her.

"Why, I'm shouting," she said in her ordinary voice.

They walked on again. Barbara was saying something but, at first, Laurel did not pay attention. She was suddenly, wonderfully, free of Marguerite — and she was giddy with relief. She was not going to have to stand there under Herb's scornful gaze. She was not going to have to remember to face front, to speak out, to look as though she were listening. Barbara would be Marguerite. Barbara had wanted to from the beginning. Laurel's family might be disappointed but she'd tell them that Miss Roe — no, that Barbara . . .

"So you're *not* going to quit!" Barbara's determined voice caught Laurel's ear at last. "I'll help you with your part. You're just being silly. Do you think Herb wasn't scared the first time he was in a play?"

"Herb scared?"

"Sure he was," Barbara said grandly. "He told me so himself last spring when we were doing *Riverside Remembers*. He shook like a jelly and he couldn't say a single word until he was prompted three times. Then, in the middle, he forgot the most important line in the play and walked off stage and left the rest of the cast just standing until the teacher sent him back in to say it."

"I don't remember that," Laurel said, so astonished to learn that Herb had ever lacked acting ability that she forgot herself for a moment.

"You wouldn't," Barbara said. She did not explain that all of this had happened when Herb was only seven years old. They had reached the Wests' front walk and she was safe from Laurel's questions.

"You're not quitting so stop thinking about it. So long, Marguerite," Barbara laughed. Leaving Laurel sputtering, she hurried into the house.

Laurel headed for home, her thoughts busy with what Barbara had told her.

If Herb had really been scared, as scared as all that, maybe Barbara was right. Maybe she, Laurel, could become an actress yet. After all, if she could learn her lines, speaking out and facing the audience wouldn't be impossible.

The wonderful relief which had spun her heart like a top left her abruptly. Barbara clearly had no intention of stepping into the part of Marguerite tomorrow. Laurel was still to be the leading lady.

"Darn!" she said to herself, trying hard to sound disgusted.

But Barbara's words sang in her. "I'll help you with your part," Barbara had said. She could not imagine what had prompted the offer. She had not yet discovered that Barbara, like herself, had had to grow up earlier than most girls, and that helping the helpless was as much a part of Barbara as it was of her. She only knew that Barbara had sounded like a friend.

She opened her own front door and stepped into the warmth and light of the hall. Lindsay, passing by, stopped and looked up at her big sister.

"What's funny?" the little girl asked.

"You!" Laurel swooped down on her and hugged her till she was breathless.

"Oo-oo, you're *cold!*" Lindsay squealed happily.

Laurel set her down and went to hang up her coat. She could still feel the smile Lindsay had noticed tugging at her mouth. She was happy because of Barbara, that was all.

Not even to herself would Laurel admit that she had been grinning because she was not going to have to admit defeat in front of Elspeth. Not yet, at least.

14

The Bravery of Butterflies

Both Laurel and Elspeth were sure, at first, that the bond between them had broken and was beyond mending. Friendship had caught them unaware and, magical though it was, they were still surprised at it when their failure to understand each other ended it. Both accepted the new hostility between them without protest. They had been at odds in the past. They had always managed to keep a polite distance from each other then. They planned to do so again.

It was harder than they had thought possible. They were roommates now. They often laughed at the same jokes without meaning to. Elspeth could not resist exclaiming over Puff as he stuffed his cheeks with peanuts, and Laurel could not help hearing and nodding. Jessica Marlowe always addressed them as though they were one. "Girls, would you clear the table." "Show the girls your drawing, Lindsay." They had the same homework and, although they did not talk about it, each knew why the other sighed deeply over her books.

As the days passed, both of them began to see that the bond had not really snapped. It had only snarled. Each of them wished, with all her heart, that the other would speak the first healing words, but neither of them was quite sure enough to begin. After twelve long, lonely days, it was straightened out in an evening.

The untangling started, surprisingly, with Lindsay telling the family about the migration of birds. She had just learned about this miracle at nursery school and she was sure that the rest of them would be as amazed and enchanted as she when they discovered where the robins had disappeared to.

"Butterflies too," James put in unexpectedly. "Butterflies go there too, Lindsay."

Lindsay sniffed scornfully and Laurel, from long habit, hurried to rescue James before he got in any deeper.

"Not butterflies, James. They're much too small and weak to go all that way. They hibernate in cocoons or something," she finished vaguely, uncertain of her facts.

Aunt Jessica contradicted her and upheld James, an experience new to Laurel.

"James is quite right," she stated flatly, leaving no room for argument.

Her head had gone up. Her cheeks grew pink. Her eyes began to gleam. She took a deep breath. The children, watching her, knew that Aunt Jessica was "off on one of her favorite things." Even Laurel, taken aback at being corrected so firmly, forgot her pricked vanity and listened with eagerness. Get Aunt Jessica started on one of her pet subjects — ballet or folk songs or coral or pioneer days in Canada — and she held you spellbound. Now the Rosses added monarch butterflies to the list.

Elspeth was as involved as her mother this time. About a year before, the two of them had read about the work of Dr. Fred A. Urquhart of the University of Toronto. Aunt Jessica had written in for information and had joined a group of amateurs who served as research assistants. She and Elspeth had been sent special numbered tags to be attached to the wings of monarch butterflies. They had read of butterflies journeying all the way from Canada to Mexico. Not only do the small, frail insects travel thousands of miles to the south but some of them may actually make the journey safely home again to Ontario.

"My teacher said that too," James said smugly, glancing sideways at Laurel.

Elspeth's animated face grew suddenly serious and even shy.

"Tell her . . . them the poem, Mother," she said.

She looked fixedly at her plate as she spoke although it was empty. Laurel knew that Elspeth had meant "her" not "them." Somehow this poem was intended for her, Laurel. Maybe, just maybe, Elspeth was asking to be friends again.

"It was written by a friend of mine after I told her about the monarchs," Aunt Jessica was explaining. "I'm afraid she's not very scientific about them . . ."

"Oh, Mother!" Elspeth protested, raising her head.

"All right, dear," Aunt Jessica said mildly. "I hope I can remember it . . ."

She began to recite, pausing now and again to correct herself.

A friendship is a fragile thing
— Like the dust of bloom on a butterfly's wing. . . .

Laurel did not understand all of the next few lines. The poet was talking about how easy it is to hurt a friendship. Laurel recognized that much — and knew it was true.

Aunt Jessica went on.

You cup your hands, try not to clutch,
But it is crippled by your touch,
By all the self-involved demands
Implicit in your closing hands. . . .

Laurel, thinking of how easily, how swiftly, the friendship between herself and Elspeth had been "crippled," only caught a phrase or two until the poet repeated:

Yes, friendship is a fragile thing
— Like the dust of bloom on a butterfly's wing.

Then, an intensity in Elspeth's face, a deeper note in Aunt Jessica's voice, made her really listen.

Yet, deep in love, there also lies
The bravery of butterflies.
Butterflies go through nights of storm
Migrating to a land that's warm.
They drift in brilliant frailty,

Testaments to mortality,
And all the while, they own the strength
To mount the wind, and come at length
Home again, their loveliness
Enduring through the journey's stress.
A treasured friendship also can
Survive the blundering of man.
Although it is a fragile thing,
It has the courage to take wing,
Dare to ride the dark, and come
Bravely home.

Dad broke the hush that followed the poem.

"That's very nice, Jessica," he said, putting down his empty coffee cup.

"Nice!" Laurel wanted to shout at him. "It's more than 'nice.'"

But Aunt Jessica gave her no time to shout anything. She got to her feet without another word of butterflies or poems.

"You girls look after these dishes," she said. "I have a job for Lindsay and James upstairs."

The two girls were alone together in the kitchen, Elspeth washing and Laurel drying and putting away. Still, the silence between them held. Laurel searched for the right words. It was her turn now.

But there were no right words, she discovered. She had waited long enough. She plunged in helter-skelter.

"You didn't want to come here, did you?" she demanded bluntly.

The question sounded wrong but it was too late to take

it back. Elspeth splashed about busily in the dishwater. All at once she gave up pretending and turned to face her cousin squarely.

"No, I didn't," she admitted, "not at first. But you didn't want me here either, did you?"

Laurel thought back. She spoke slowly but she told the truth. It was a time when only the truth would do.

"No, I guess not — but I felt differently about it that very first day."

"Did you?" Elspeth half whispered. "So did I. Everything was different . . ."

Then she began to laugh. Laurel did not understand.

"Don't you remember?" Elspeth sobered for an instant. Then she twinkled again. "That was what I said on that night when we . . . when we got mad at each other. I said my whole life here was 'different' and you said '*your* whole life!'"

"But I thought you meant . . ." Laurel began.

They were off then, interrupting each other, laughing at their own stupidity, explaining themselves. They were still at it when they went to bed. Aunt Jessica had to call up, "Turn that light out, girls, and go to sleep."

There was so much to get sorted out — how each of them had felt about the other's clothes, how they had felt about the shift in rooms, how Laurel had felt about Briarhill . . .

"Elspeth and Laurel," Aunt Jessica came halfway up the stairs this time, "stop that chattering and go to sleep this minute. It's nearly eleven o'clock."

After that they had to talk in whispers.

"You know," Laurel said at last, grateful for the darkness which made secrets easier to share, "I never had a friend before — not like you and Maureen."

"Maureen!" Elspeth squealed right out loud. "She's not my friend. It's our mothers who are friends. Whenever Mother has Mrs. Claremont over, she always drags Maureen along and I have to be polite to her. She's horrible. She talks about nothing but boys, boys, boys — and I know for a fact that no boy would be caught dead speaking to her."

"How about Sally though — and Joanne?" Laurel asked.

Elspeth explained about Sally living in the same apartment building and staying with the Marlowes when her mother was away. Joanne was one of her cousins on her father's side, "but she's seventeen!" Elspeth said, "and she thinks she's twenty-two! She calls me 'little Elspeth.'"

Laurel thought back to the bits of Aunt Jessica's letters which, in the days when she had had only James, had made her feel so alone. "Elspeth and Sally are off to a movie." "Joanne is here and the girls are watching television." "Maureen and Elspeth are going skating and I have to drive them so I must run." Why, it had been nothing, nothing at all. She and Elspeth had discovered friendship together.

They did not go to sleep till well after midnight.

15

Laurel Cannot Help

Laurel, Lindsay, James and Elspeth were watching television. The heroine's horse had run away with her and Lindsay got so excited she jumped to her feet and started jigging up and down.

"Lindsay, sit DOWN!" Laurel said automatically but she did not crane her neck to see around the bobbing figure. She was so comfortable in Dad's big chair with Puff curled on her lap. She stroked his silky fur softly, absentmindedly.

She was thinking about the play. She had spent the afternoon at Barbara's going over her lines. Barbara had been stern with her. They had gone right to work the moment Laurel arrived and had not stopped until Laurel had to go home for supper. But she knew them now! For the tenth time that evening, she went over Marguerite's longest speech. It played smoothly inside her head, the words coming without a pause. Just wait! Just wait till Herb heard her!

"Lind-say!" Aunt Jessica called.

Lindsay pretended not to hear.

"Lindsay Ross, it's high time you were in bed." Aunt Jessica came to the top of the basement stairs.

"But the girls aren't up there yet," Lindsay said feebly.

"You know perfectly well that the girls don't have to go to bed for a couple of hours yet. Hurry up, Lindsay. That program's over and you can't watch another."

"I'm coming up in just a couple of minutes myself," Elspeth said casually.

Laurel, who had been wondering what happened to the girl on the runaway horse, now looked at her cousin with astonishment.

"But I thought we were going to watch that movie on Channel Six," she said.

"I'm tired," Elspeth said briefly. "And I'm reading a good book."

Laurel, following Elspeth's gaze, saw Lindsay brighten. Without further protest, the small girl trotted up the stairs and took Aunt Jessica's hand.

"Oh," Laurel said, understanding all at once.

To think Elspeth had realized that Lindsay would be frightened up there alone in the little room without them next door! Yet Elspeth had come only two weeks ago. Laurel stroked Puff harder than she meant to. He wriggled out from under her hard hand and bustled away into the corner of the chair, headfirst.

"Oh, *no!*" Laurel wailed.

"What's wrong?" Elspeth asked.

Laurel simply pointed. Elspeth gasped.

"Not Puff!"

"It must have been Puff," Laurel nodded.

He had eaten a hole right through her gray skirt.

"Didn't you feel him doing it?" Elspeth demanded.

Laurel shook her head. Suddenly she realized that the hamster was escaping over the edge of the chair. She grabbed him and held him up in front of her and looked him in the eye.

"How could you be such a sneak?" she asked him.

She was not holding him comfortably and he did not enjoy that space beneath himself. His back paws scrabbled on thin air.

"Laurie, don't. You'll hurt him!"

Laurel lowered him to her lap again.

"You're going right straight back to your cage, Mr. Monster-Hamster!" she scolded. "Lindsay was right about you."

At the same moment she and Elspeth realized that something was wrong. Despite all their hullabaloo, James had not moved. A physics lecture had come on in place of the cowboy show, but James had not switched to another channel. He stayed on the low footstool. He was bunched up until his chin almost rested on his knees. He appeared to be watching the lecturer intently, but neither Laurel nor Elspeth could understand the equations which the man was now putting on the chalkboard.

Both girls were silent for a moment, looking at James's back. They had forgotten Puff and the damage to Laurel's skirt. Even their sudden, complete stillness did not make James turn his head to look at them. Through the drone of the lecturer's voice, they could hear the small boy's ragged breathing. Across the room, they both saw his narrow shoulders shake.

"I'll take Puff up for you," Elspeth said softly, reaching for him.

Laurel handed him over. Her eyes met her cousin's.

"He's crying," Elspeth mouthed.

Laurel nodded.

Elspeth tiptoed out of the room, leaving Laurel alone with her brother.

The lecturer's voice filled the room but neither the boy nor the girl heard what was being so carefully explained. Laurel was afraid. Her mouth had grown dry, her palms damp. She licked her lips and swallowed. She scrubbed her hands hard against her skirt. She tried desperately to think what she ought to do, what she was going to say.

Two weeks before, she would not have needed words. Two weeks ago, James would not have sat there crying, with his back to her. Somehow that fortnight had changed everything. He was not entirely hers any longer.

Laurel had thought of him as Aunt Jessica's now. Aunt Jessica took him back and forth to and from school. Aunt Jessica helped him get ready for bed. Aunt Jessica was teaching him how to get undressed without help and he now bathed himself. Laurel, going by the door, had heard her aunt saying, "Start at the top button, James," and "Pull both laces at once or it will knot." Aunt Jessica let James watch television instead of reading him a story. Why Laurel had not been alone with James since that first night when he had moved downstairs and she had tucked him in and told him about Puff!

"James . . ." Laurel started. Her voice creaked rustily and she had to clear her throat.

James bent his face right down onto his knees. He wrapped his skinny arms around his head. Laurel stared helplessly at the little hump he made. What was she to do? Then she heard him sob and, without stopping to think further, she jumped up and went to him.

He kicked at first and slapped wildly at her but she paid no attention. She hauled him over to Dad's chair, pulled him onto her lap, held onto him for dear life and began to scold him roundly.

"You nut!" she stormed at him. "Now just stop that. I said STOP THAT and sit still. What's got into you anyway? Here, use this Kleenex. All right. That's better. Now you sit up, James, and tell me what's the matter with you — and quit bawling while you do it."

James rubbed the tears away. He gave one final hiccoughy sob, one last almighty sniffle. The old Laurel, the bossy Laurel, the Laurel who had taken care of him ever since he could remember, his Laurel was miraculously back. He told her what was wrong.

"She says I have to go to school myself from now on. She says . . ."

"Don't you start crying again," Laurel warned him sharply as his voice wavered and broke. "She" was obviously Aunt Jessica. Laurel bit her lip.

"She says that now I know the way, I have to learn to

. . . to act my age. She says . . . time I stuck up for my-self . . ."

"Do you know the way?" Laurel asked.

He tried to evade her steady eyes but she pulled his chin around.

"Do you?" she insisted.

"Yes," he said wretchedly. "I took her all the way there twice and back too."

There was silence. I was going to teach him that, Laurel thought. . . . And there's the play . . . but Mama wouldn't want . . . Barbara could be Marguerite . . .

"James," she said, holding onto his arms so tightly he squirmed, "you have to understand. Do you want to have to walk to school with your sister when you're twelve and thirteen?"

James clearly saw nothing wrong with that idea so she hurried on. She knew she was sounding exactly like Aunt Jessica, but, after all, Aunt Jessica was right.

"You're just being a big baby," she finished. She was almost shouting. He was so still. His chin was down on his chest. She took a deep breath and got ready to go on, but suddenly he wriggled out of her clutch. "Aunt Jessica's calling me," he mumbled. He tripped over the edge of the rug on his way to the stairs.

Laurel, watching him stumble up the steps, blinked back tears.

"I can't help it. He has to learn," she whispered angrily.

The next morning when she went into the bathroom to brush her teeth, she saw the wet sheet and his pajamas soaking in the tub.

16

Who's Alice?

While they were dressing, she explained it to Elspeth.

"I'll just have to walk with him somehow," she decided. "If I meet him at the corner, your mother won't know. It's these boys, you see. Oh, Elspeth, you should have seen him that day!"

She shuddered remembering James lying in the snow, hearing again his thin, lost cry.

"Barbara would really like to play Marguerite, I know," Laurel went on, sounding forlorn in spite of herself.

"Nonsense," Elspeth said calmly.

Laurel stared at her cousin.

"Wha-at?" she stammered.

"You were right last night and you know it. Mother's right too," Elspeth sounded so sure. She was brushing her hair vigorously and Laurel could hear it crackle with electricity as she talked.

"But suppose those boys are waiting for him? Suppose they chase him again and . . ."

"Suppose they don't," Elspeth said sensibly, putting down her brush. "Suppose nobody bothers him and, in a day or so, he gets over being scared. Suppose he even makes a friend of his own."

"But they half killed him!" Laurel was indignant.

"We'll follow him then."

Laurel's mouth dropped open, but Elspeth was not her mother's daughter for nothing. She had the whole plan worked out in a matter of seconds.

The two girls would give James a headstart. Then they would "shadow" him like detectives all the way to school. Elspeth would do it herself on the way home and Laurel could stay behind for play practice.

"You know you want to be in that play," she reminded Laurel, who was still hesitating. Then she said quietly, "Look, Laurel, didn't he ever wet the bed before these boys scared him? I thought you said it happened every week or so. Did you always get into a tizzy like this before we came?"

Laurel had to think a long way back. Somehow that seemed like another life. Slowly, half reluctantly, she shook her head.

"Well then," Elspeth said — and it was settled.

It was easier than Laurel had thought it could be. James kept his eyes fixed on the road ahead. He looked small and defenseless, trudging along a block ahead of them. When

he turned the corner near the school, Laurel was tempted
to dash after him. She was sure that the moment he got out
of sight, danger would overtake him. But Elspeth held her
back. When they edged their way around the corner, there
he was, safe and sound, crossing the playground. They
watched until he disappeared into the school building.
Then, and only then, did Laurel remember Barbara.

"I promised to meet Barbara this morning," she cried in
consternation.

"She was behind us. I saw her when we were about a
block past her place. Wait, Laurel. What are you going to
tell her?"

Laurel, who had been on the point of rushing off to find
Barbara and explain, stopped.

"I'll say that James . . . that we had to . . ." she
floundered.

"She must have seen us," Elspeth said reasonably. "We
weren't even *with* James. I guess we must have looked a bit
queer sometimes, when we thought James was going to
turn around, and we ducked behind those trees. She must
have thought we were hiding . . ."

"There she is," Laurel said. "I'll think of something."

She hurried toward Barbara but the other girl saw her
coming. Before Laurel could attempt an explanation, Barbara had turned away. She ran into the classroom. Laurel
halted, undecided.

"Maybe she thought we were hiding from *her*," Elspeth
guessed, catching up.

"She couldn't have," Laurel returned, but she was not
sure.

Barbara did not look up when the other two slid into their seats. Laurel took a deep breath and leaned toward her.

"Barbara, listen."

"I'm busy," Barbara said coldly.

"But it's about . . ."

Laurel stopped short. Margaret Muir was listening too and watching her with curious eyes. John Dickson was leaning forward, not missing a word. She could just hear his guffaw if he were to learn that she had had to watch James all the way to school. He'd be calling her Dick Tracy or something.

"Laurel," Elspeth whispered, warningly.

"I know," returned Laurel. She tried not to look at Barbara all morning. The first chance she got alone with her, she would make the whole thing clear.

The chance did not come that day. When school was over and Elspeth had gone, Barbara asked Miss Roe if she needed to stay. She knew her lines and her mother was not well. The teacher let her go.

Herb's eyes widened as Laurel sailed through her part. But without Barbara there to see and share in the triumph, Laurel felt cheated.

They watched for Barbara the next morning but they missed her. It was two days before they learned by accident that she was walking to school by a new way.

Miss Roe heard Barbara run through Marguerite's lines on Thursday and told her that she need not keep coming to practice until dress rehearsal.

One afternoon Laurel did manage to catch up with her

in the hall between periods. She looked around hastily to see who was in earshot. She couldn't say James was mentally retarded. Even the doctor had not known for certain. But, perhaps, if she could put it in some roundabout way . . .

"Barbara," she began breathlessly, "suppose you had a brother or sister who needed you, who was . . . different. . . ."

Barbara drew back. Her eyes seemed to grow bigger all at once and something in her taut face made Laurel pause. Before Laurel could finish her sentence, Barbara fled from her, banging into people as she went.

Laurel stood, stupefied, watching the other girl plunge away.

"You'd think the devil himself was after her," she thought, quoting Mama. But she was not the devil. What had come over Barbara?

The next morning, Barbara asked Miss Roe if she could move to a vacant place nearer the front of the room. When Miss Roe agreed, Barbara came back and emptied her desk without a glance at either Laurel or Elspeth.

Laurel almost gave up then. She sat in her bedroom that night after school and thought about it. Suddenly, unbidden, Aunt Jessica's poem about the monarch butterflies came to her.

> *Yes, friendship is a fragile thing*
> *— Like the dust of bloom on a butterfly's wing.*
> *Yet, deep in love, there also lies*
> *The bravery of butterflies . . .*

She had copied out the poem and she got it out of her desk drawer and read over the rest of it. She stopped and reread the last lines.

> *A treasured friendship also can*
> *Survive the blundering of man.*
> *Although it is a fragile thing,*
> *It has the courage to take wing,*
> *Dare to ride the dark, and come*
> *Bravely home.*

She and Barbara had been friends. The trouble between them must be just such a foolish misunderstanding as the trouble between her and Elspeth had been. That time Elspeth had held friendship out again through this poem. Elspeth had had "the courage to take wing."

She had already tried, Laurel reminded herself. But monarchs did not turn back when they encountered a storm. She would try again.

She phoned the Wests on Friday night when Aunt Jessica was upstairs putting the children to bed and Dad was in the basement watching a special on TV.

She heard Mrs. West call Barbara.

"Ask who it is," Barbara said. Laurel pressed her ear tighter to the receiver so that she would hear.

"It's Laurel Ross. She told me so. Hurry up, Barb."

"Tell her I'm not home."

"I will do no such thing," Mrs. West said. "You just get over here and talk to her. Don't be so silly, Barbie."

"She knows about Alice," Barbara stormed.

Mrs. West must have put her hand over the mouthpiece

then, for Laurel caught only one more snippet of conversation.

"But, Barbie, we're not ashamed of Alice . . ."

Then Barbara spoke directly into Laurel's ear.

"I'm sorry," she said, her voice icy. "Barbara is not at home."

The receiver slammed into place.

"Who's Alice?" Laurel asked baffled, rubbing her ear.

"Search me," Elspeth shrugged.

Laurel's temper flared then.

"For crying out loud, who does she think she is?" she exploded. "I haven't done one single, solitary thing to her except forget to pick her up last Monday morning."

"I know," Elspeth said absently. "But I wonder who Alice is."

"Who cares?" Laurel banged out of her chair. She passed Lindsay on her way to the stairs. Lindsay looked up at her older sister whose face was like a thundercloud. Then she looked gravely at Elspeth, still standing by the phone.

"Let her stew in her own juice," she advised.

Elspeth doubled up with laughter. Alice was forgotten.

17

Leading Lady

Alice remained a mystery but as the days flew past, Laurel had no time left to wonder about her. She almost forgot the scrap of conversation she had overheard on the phone as she was caught up in the rush of getting ready for Christmas.

It was going to be a queer Christmas. The children did not speak of its queerness when the family was together but each of them felt it more and more as Christmas neared.

On the Tuesday before the holiday, Aunt Jessica sent Laurel to look for Lindsay.

"I sent her to get the Scotch tape," she said, "and she hasn't come back. It's right there on the shelf in your Dad's closet. I saw it there myself last night. It's with the box of wrapping paper and stickers."

Lindsay had found the Scotch tape. She had it in her hand but she had not come out of the closet. Laurel, opening the door wider, discovered her with her face buried in Mama's blue wool dress. She was crying.

These tears were no mystery. The sight of her mother's clothes hanging there, pushed over to make room for James's shirts and good pants and blazer, brought a lump into Laurel's own throat.

"Come on, Linnet," she said gently, pulling her away.

"I don't want it to be Christmas without Mama," Lindsay sobbed. "I got her some perfume with a picture of violets on it. I don't want Daddy to take it to the hospital. I want to give it to her myself!"

"I know," Laurel choked.

She had bought her mother a new Blue Mountain teapot. It had meant skimping on the rest of the family but Mama had seemed so much more important than the rest. And now, she wouldn't be able to see Mama's face when she unwrapped it.

"We're being silly," she managed, scolding herself and Lindsay together. "What matters is that Mama gets well — it shouldn't be long now. Maybe she'll be home for New Year's."

Lindsay was not comforted. New Year's Day had no meaning for a four-year-old. Then Laurel had an idea.

"I know somebody who's just as lonesome as you are, Lindsay," she coaxed. "And you could make him feel so much better. He's missing his Mama too, and he's lots sadder than you are because he used to live with seven brothers and sisters but now he has to live all alone."

Puff did not look particularly unhappy when the two girls peered into his cage. Laurel touched the bars and he only curled up more tightly.

"He's sleeping!" Lindsay said doubtfully. "Are you sure he's lonely?"

Laurel glanced at the windows. It was dark. Puff should be ready to waken. She opened the top of the cage and lifted him out carefully. He gave his mammoth yawn and Lindsay giggled.

"Let me hold him, Laurel," she begged.

Lindsay was forever wanting to hold Puff. But she was so afraid he would escape that she clutched him much too tightly each time he moved.

"You go get him a cookie and then you can hold him." Laurel promised.

After all, he did really belong to her.

When Lindsay returned, cookie in hand, Laurel sat her down and put the tiny creature on her lap. He was busy munching the cookie so he did not go exploring.

"Where is his Mama?" Lindsay wanted to know. "She isn't dead, is she?" There was such horror in her voice that Laurel understood that her little sister had been frightened that Mama would die and never come home.

"No, no, goofy. She's over at Barbara West's." Laurel explained hastily. "She's perfectly fine," she added.

Younger brothers and sisters were a worry, she mused, as she watched Lindsay's little squarish hand stroking Puff's smooth fur. She had said as much once to Barbara and Elspeth when the three of them had been walking to school together.

"You don't know how lucky you two are being only children!" she had sighed.

Barbara had made no reply at all, but perhaps she had felt that Elspeth said it for her when Elspeth flashed back:

"Lucky! You're the one who's lucky and you don't even know it!"

She should have realized right then and there that Elspeth enjoyed being part of a family, that Elspeth and she had been talking at cross-purposes that long-ago night when they had come so close to quarreling. Now it was she and Barbara who had somehow lost touch with each other.

"Laurel, he's getting away!" Lindsay squeaked.

Laurel rescued Puff and sent Lindsay to Aunt Jessica with the Scotch tape. She could hear their voices in the kitchen.

"Where on earth have you been, Miss Ross?" Aunt Jessica wanted to know.

"I was comforting Puff," Lindsay explained.

"My heavens, what next!" Aunt Jessica exclaimed.

Elspeth, who had been practicing, came bounding up the stairs.

"Done, done, done!" she sang, spinning around.

"Was James okay today?" Laurel wanted to know when they were by themselves.

"Sure, he was," Elspeth said. "After the holidays, I think we could quit following . . ."

Laurel turned away from the sudden lost look on her cousin's face. "Tomorrow's dress rehearsal," she announced.

"As though you haven't been telling us for weeks," Elspeth scoffed.

Neither of them could put into words the truth which Elspeth had just brought home to them both. After the holidays, Elspeth would be back at Briarhill.

"I wonder if, someday, we'll forget this Christmas, Marguerite," Nicholas said, as the rest of the family capered around gaily in the background.

"Don't be foolish, Nick," Marguerite answered, tipping back her head to look up at him. She caught his hands and whirled him around suddenly. "Why, we never really knew what Christmas was all about — until today."

"Merry Christmas, dear Marguerite," Nicholas loosed his hands and made her a courtly bow.

"Oh, Nick, Merry Merry Christmas," Marguerite said fervently, sweeping him a beautiful curtsy.

Laurel came up as the curtain went down. It was over. She had even managed to curtsy without wobbling. She had only to be prompted once and even then she had really remembered the line herself just as Miss Roe's voice came softly from the wings to remind her. Best of all, most amazing of all, she had forgotten about Laurel Ross entirely and she had had no trouble putting feeling in. How could she help sounding like Marguerite when she really was Marguerite, long skirts, pantaloons and all.

The curtain went up again and the players took their curtain calls. They peered over the footlights, looking for their families. There they were, even Lindsay, clapping as though they'd never stop. James looked lost. He was clapping too but Laurel was sure that he did not know why.

She moved forward with Herb to take a special bow, just for the two of them.

Barbara was in the front row. Laurel saw her clearly in the light spilling over from the stage. Barbara was not clapping.

18

Christmas Eve

"No more *pencils!*" James sang. "No more *books* . . ."

One more day to go! Last minute shopping to do! Laurel trudged home with parcels piled up to her chin. In front of the Wests' a car was pulling in. Laurel, passing, heard Barbara say clearly:

"We're home, Alice!"

"Home," a strange voice echoed. It sounded like a little girl's voice . . . almost.

Whoever Alice was, she was there right now, but Laurel had gone by the Wests' front walk. She was balancing a small box on top of the stack with her chin. If she turned, she would have to turn entirely around or the whole lot would topple. And that would be staring.

To keep on walking toward home was one of the hardest things Laurel Ross ever did.

"Elspeth," she gasped, bursting into their room and confronting her cousin. "Alice is at Barbara's house."

Elspeth was interested but no help. There was no reason to go over. Barbara had made it clear that they were not wanted. They walked by a couple of times, but the house just sat there and told no secrets.

"Maybe you were imagining things," Elspeth teased. "Just think! Tomorrow is Christmas Day!"

Laurel was possessed by wild excitement. She whirled around and around on the snowy street.

"What's come over you?" Elspeth grabbed at her and pulled her to a halt. "What made you do that?"

"Christmas!" Laurel gasped, jerking away from Elspeth and beginning to run in circles. "Just Christmas!"

"We're too old to act that crazy," Elspeth told her. Then she gave in and they danced down the street together.

They hung their stockings up right after supper.

Lindsay peered up the chimney anxiously.

"It's big enough," Laurel told her. "I promise you it's big enough."

Then she saw her father putting on his coat.

"But, Dad," she called, suddenly as young as Lindsay, "you always read ' 'Twas the Night Before Christmas' to us and we didn't sing the carols."

He halted, his face blank.

"I can't tonight, honey. Something has come up," he said. "You read it to the others."

"But, Dad," Laurel cried after him, "it's Christmas Eve! . . ."

He was gone. She turned and faced the other children.

"Well, don't just stand there. Where's the book?" she demanded gruffly.

"I want Daddy to read it, not you," Lindsay protested. "You don't make it exciting enough."

"Just sit down and listen to your sister, Lindsay," Aunt Jessica said unexpectedly from the kitchen, her voice tart. "If you don't want to hear her read, you can march right up to bed."

"I'm going to get a walkie-talkie," James said for the twentieth time since supper.

"Would you like me to read it?" Elspeth offered hesitatingly.

"Yes, I want *Elspeth* to read it," Lindsay clamored at once. "And you are not going to get a walkie-talkie, James. Daddy says they're too expensive."

"Leave him alone," Laurel snapped. She grabbed the book and shoved it at Elspeth. She picked Lindsay up and plunked her down on the couch with orders to be quiet and listen.

Lindsay sat with her head hanging. Elspeth began to read shakily. Laurel sat jammed crookedly into her father's chair. She heard Lindsay gulp. Aunt Jessica was rattling dishes in the kitchen. If only she'd come in here and . . . Laurel wasn't sure what she wanted her aunt to do.

"I want Mama," she thought desperately. "Oh, I do want Mama."

All her memories of other Christmas Eves melted into one golden image, much lovelier than any one of them. They had always been a family on this one night. James had fitted in. Tonight James was not even listening. He was looking at pictures in a horror comic. Laurel reached out and snatched it out of his hand.

"A fine thing to be looking at on Christmas Eve, James Ross," she told him, interrupting Elspeth in the middle of, "More rapid than eagles, his coursers they came."

James's face puckered. Laurel, hating him suddenly, pushed the comic down behind her where he could not get it. "Either you pay attention to Elspeth or go to bed," she commanded.

Now they were all unhappy. Lindsay was crying quietly. James howled at the top of his voice. Elspeth, who had been doing her level best with the poem, looked accusingly at Laurel. Laurel stared stonily at all three of them.

"Bed, every last one of you," Aunt Jessica ordered from the doorway. "Never mind arguing, Laurel. I know the time perfectly well. I also know that, for some reason, you're exhausted. You won't be fit to live with tomorrow if you don't get some rest."

It was just past eight o'clock.

"Mama wouldn't . . . " Laurel started.

"Your mother is not here just now," Aunt Jessica said crisply. "Go on, all of you. James, stop that bellowing. I'll be up in a minute. If you two girls aren't sleepy, you may read in your room."

"If Dad comes home . . ." Laurel tried once more.

"He won't," Aunt Jessica said briefly. Was she smiling? No, Laurel could not believe she could be that cruel. She looked again. Aunt Jessica was her most severe self.

By nine o'clock, the four of them were in bed. Elspeth hid behind a book. Laurel was glad. Everything had been spoiled. If Christmas Day were going to be like this, Laurel hoped it would never come.

Suddenly she remembered herself whirling down the street, crazy with Christmas joy. She snapped out the light over her bed and buried her face in the pillow.

"Mama," she wept. "Oh, Mama."

19

Santa Claus Is Downstairs!

"Laurel . . . Laurel!"

"Okay," Laurel said crossly, out of a fog of sleep. She moved over to make room for Lindsay. Her eyes stayed shut.

"Laurel, listen!"

"What in the world . . ." Laurel began, but Lindsay's excited whisper broke in again.

"Laurel, Santa Claus is downstairs. Really! Listen!"

Laurel was awake now. She got up on one elbow. She looked at the luminous dial on her clock. It was past midnight — and, sure enough, there were sounds coming up from downstairs. A thump . . . somebody walking . . .

"That's his big black boots," Lindsay hissed.

There was a quick burst of laughter. "Shhh!" somebody said.

But now, Laurel's heart was pounding as hard as Lindsay's. She scrambled out of bed.

"What are we going to do?" Lindsay squeaked. Laurel, reaching to steady herself on Lindsay's shoulder, while she put on her slippers, found the little girl shivering violently.

"Are you cold — or scared?"

"I'm cold," Lindsay retorted. Then she added in a voice so low Laurel hardly heard her *"and* scared."

"Laurel Ross," Elspeth said, right out loud. She had reared up and, in the faint starry light, Laurel could see her staring at the two of them. "What are you doing?"

Lindsay darted over to Elspeth. "Santa Claus," she babbled. "He's downstairs. Listen, Elspeth. Just listen."

"You're both crazy," Elspeth said, but now she was whispering too.

Deep silence floated up the stairs to their straining ears.

"There's nobody there," Elspeth told them, settling back.

"Yes, there is," Laurel was pulling on her bathrobe. She wanted to dash out of the room and see for herself, but the hour and the darkness and the stillness made her wait. Besides, it was Lindsay who had heard the noise first. Lindsay had to be with her. And Elspeth too. Suddenly, clearly, she saw the look in Elspeth's eyes when she had bravely started reading "A Visit from Saint Nicholas" aloud. It had not meant anything special to Elspeth. She had just been trying to help fill in the loneliness, the emptiness where she knew Laurel, James and Lindsay were lost.

"Elspeth, come *on!*"

Something urgent in Laurel's voice, a note Elspeth had

never heard before, brought the other girl hurrying out of bed and into her slippers.

"If he hears you, he'll disappear," Lindsay said. She was almost in tears. Laurel took her hand and the world righted itself.

They tiptoed down the stairs and into the living room. Dad was just depositing the sleeping James on the living room couch.

"I knew it!" Laurel screamed. "I knew it! Oh, Dad!"

"But that's not Santa Claus. He hasn't come at all," Lindsay said, bewildered.

"In the bedroom, Laurie," Dad said — and grinned.

"But Santa Claus doesn't go in bedrooms . . ." Lindsay started.

"Come *on!*" Laurel shouted, whirling and dragging Lindsay with her. Then, groaning, she halted.

"James . . ." she implored.

"I'm bringing him," Dad said. "Come on, boy. Your sister was too smart for us."

Hubbub followed — laughing, crying, hugging, kissing, shrieking, explaining, everybody joining in at once.

"Lindsay woke me. She thought Santa . . ."

"We were going to surprise you. I only knew myself yesterday . . ."

"Be careful of your mother's cast, James . . ."

"I couldn't believe my ears. I was half asleep but I heard you laugh . . ."

"When Dr. Fullbright gave in, we arranged to bring her to Marcus's right after supper . . ."

"I was supposed to be an extra Christmas present under your tree . . ."

Finally only Lindsay managed to make herself heard above the general din.

"But, Laurel," she piped, peering around. "That's not Santa Claus. That's Mama!"

How they laughed then!

Mama, noticing Elspeth standing back in the doorway, called, "Niece, come and give me a kiss."

James suddenly announced, "I have to go to the toilet," and scooted off.

Aunt Jessica fetched a sweater and draped it around Lindsay's shoulders. The little girl was shivering with sheer excitement.

"We must all go to bed," Dad said, sounding younger than he had in a long time, "and give Santa Claus a chance. Don't worry, Linnet. He'll make it yet. You know what 'The Year Without a Santa Claus' says — 'Yearly, newly, faithfully, truly, somehow . . .'"

" 'Santa Claus always comes!' " Lindsay chanted.

Her eyes were glowing. Her cheeks were like pink roses. Her fair curls stood up in a soft, rumpled halo.

"She looks like a Christmas angel," Laurel said, her voice soft with wonder. Then she scooped her small sister up and squeezed her. "Too bad she never acts like one," she growled.

Lindsay, hearing the love beneath the growl, twined her arms around Laurel's neck and hugged her back.

"Bed, right this minute," Dad ordered, shooing them toward the door.

"All right, James. One more kiss for your mother. I have a special bed fixed up for you on the couch."

"But James will see Santa Claus if Daddy lets him sleep on the couch," Lindsay objected as the girls climbed the stairs. "If he sees him, Santa Claus will just vanish, Laurel, really."

"James will be sound asleep before Santa Claus gets around to our chimney," Laurel promised.

"I won't be," Lindsay's eyes were wide open. Nothing remotely like this had ever happened to her before. "I'm going to stay awake till morning. I'll just never shut my eyes at all."

Laurel felt sure she would not sleep a wink herself, but she was older than Lindsay. She remembered other times when she had been positive she would stay awake all night.

"We'll both be fast asleep in no time," she told the smaller girl.

Goodness, I sounded like a grown-up, she thought, not pleased at the idea.

"Laurel," Elspeth said, when Lindsay was in bed, if not asleep, "it's Christmas Day!"

"Why, so it is," Laurel said. "Elspeth . . ."

"What?" Elspeth asked when the other paused.

Laurel wanted to say, "I'm sorry I was so awful earlier. I'm terribly sorry you're going away next week. I wish you were my sister."

"Merry Christmas, Elspeth," said Laurel.

20

Alice

Laurel told herself afterwards that she should have guessed right away. But she didn't. When Elspeth came flying to tell her that Puff was missing from his cage, the two of them began an exhaustive search of the house. Even when Aunt Jessica announced it was suppertime and they gathered for a meal of Christmas leftovers and Lindsay did not appear, Laurel did not connect the two.

Perhaps she would have, in a moment, but the phone rang first. It was Mrs. West asking for Laurel.

"Lindsay is here, Laurel," she explained. "She has apparently got the notion that your hamster is homesick for his mother. I can't bring myself to tell her about Barbara's hamster," she added in a low voice.

What about Barbara's hamster? Laurel wondered, but did not need to ask for Mrs. West went right on.

"Barbara has felt so upset about her. It has been over two weeks since she died but we can't seem to comfort Barbara . . . Anyway, Lindsay won't be persuaded that Puff — is that what you call him?"

"Yes," Laurel got in.

"She won't be persuaded that Puff is perfectly happy at your place. She says you told her he was lonely. Do you think you could convince her, dear? She's getting a bit upset."

"I'll be right over," Laurel said hastily.

She flung on her coat, explaining as she got ready.

"I'll come too," Elspeth jumped up to follow suit.

"No, James, not you," Dad said firmly as James began to slide off his chair.

When Mrs. West opened the door, Laurel could hear Lindsay, her voice shrill, saying, "But I *know* he wants his mama!"

"Oh Lindsay, he does not," Barbara was saying. "And don't hold him so tightly. You'll squash him."

"Why has she got Goldilocks? I want her," said another voice.

"It's not Goldilocks, Alice. This is another hamster," Barbara said. She sounded as though she had said all of these things before.

Alice! The other two girls glanced at each other. Then Laurel hurried into the Wests' living room.

"Let me have Puff, Lindsay," she said quietly to her little sister.

Lindsay handed him over but her bottom lip stuck out stubbornly.

"I brought him home to his mama, Laurel," she said. "He's lonely."

"Who's that?" asked the big girl whom Laurel did not know.

Mrs. West spoke quietly.

"This is Barbara's big sister Alice," she explained to the girls. "Alice has come home for Christmas. Alice, these girls are Laurel Ross and Elspeth . . . Marlowe, isn't it?"

Elspeth nodded.

The big girl got up and came over to peer at Puff. She was sixteen or seventeen years old. She looked a little like Barbara except that she wore glasses and she had longer hair. She moved awkwardly and she spoke too loudly. She slurred her words a little. She smiled widely at Laurel.

"Is he yours?" she asked. "Not Barbara's?"

"He's mine," Laurel told her.

Why, Alice was like James, only more so. Laurel, who had long ago learned what James could and could not grasp, knew suddenly that Alice, although she was older than James, was even younger in her ability to understand things.

"I got a new dress," Alice said.

Her smile was friendly. She put her arm loosely around Laurel's shoulders.

"I got stockings too and I got a record."

Her attention was caught by the hamster, burrowing into the crook of Laurel's elbow.

"What's his name?" she asked.

"His name is Puff," Laurel said evenly.

She liked Alice. It would have been hard not to. She

was like an overgrown puppy, joyfully wagging his tail at a stranger. Laurel looked across at Barbara. Barbara's face was set, as cold as granite. Laurel withdrew herself gently from Alice's circling arm.

"Lindsay," she said quickly, turning from Barbara's sister to her own, "Mama wants you to come home for supper. Maybe Puff wants to come with us. Wait and I'll ask him."

She held Puff up close to her cheek and inquired whether or not he wanted to go home to his cage. Puff seemed to understand his part for he suddenly stuck his little head into Laurel's hair, right up against her ear.

"What did he say, Laurie? What did he say?"

"Now that Mama has come home, he isn't lonely any more," Laurel said firmly. "He wants to go right back to his cage."

Lindsay accepted that. She wanted to go home herself, now that Mama was there. They started for the door.

"Well done, Laurel," Mrs. West said softly.

"Don't go away," Alice wailed. "I didn't show you my dress. I want to show you my new dress and . . ."

"Mother, please make her stop," Barbara said.

"All right, Alice, they'll come another time and see your dress," Mrs. West said gently. "They have to go home for supper now."

"What's wrong with her, Laurel?" Elspeth asked, when they were clear of the Wests' yard.

"I think . . . she's retarded," Laurel said slowly. "I never knew Barbara had a sister. I'm sure she doesn't live with them usually."

Then she remembered Mrs. Webster speaking of Alice, long ago. What had she said — that Alice and Barbara both loved animals — that Alice was a relative of the Wests.

The two girls were still discussing Alice when they got to the table. Aunt Jessica knew some of the answers. Alice had lived with her family when the Wests had lived in Toronto. She had attended a special school for children who were severely retarded. But there was no such school, as yet, in Riverside.

"I think Mrs. West felt that having Alice at home wasn't fair to Barbara or Alice now that they're both in their teens. She was telling me about it last week when I took back her recipe for fruitcake. Alice is up in the Provincial Residential School at Orillia now. She's happy there, Mrs. West says."

"You mean people send retarded children away somewhere?" Laurel was shocked.

"Hold on, Laurel," her father said. "That is the kind of thing it is dangerous to generalize about. One family might decide to do one thing and another family decide to do just the opposite, and neither of them would necessarily be wrong. The Wests kept Alice with them for a long time apparently, and they have chosen what they think is best for her, I'm sure. Did she look happy?"

"Yes," Laurel admitted, remembering Alice's friendly face. "Happier than Barbara."

"Well, there you are. It isn't easy, whatever you do. I suppose the important thing to remember is that each person matters and must be considered and planned for. Anyway, we'll know about James on Tuesday," he finished, half under his breath.

James had finished eating before the girls got home and was downstairs watching television. Laurel looked at her father. So he, too, had been thinking about James as he talked!

"Gracious, John, I've never heard you make such a long speech before," Aunt Jessica commented, pouring another cup of coffee for him.

"I told you he had hidden depths, Jess, when I married him," Mama laughed from her place on the couch.

Yet, under their banter, Laurel caught an anxious sound. Laurel looked at James's empty chair and wished with all her heart that Tuesday had come and gone.

When Dad brought James home on Tuesday afternoon, the boy looked younger somehow, as though he had slipped back into being the James who needed his coat undone.

"I did everything right," he bragged loudly. "I asked the man and he said I was perfect."

His eyes were so worried that Laurel patted his hand and said, "I'm sure he did, James."

But when Dr. Fullbright talked with Dad about the findings of the Clinic staff, it turned out Aunt Jessica had been right. James was "mentally retarded." He was not severely retarded like Alice West. He was "educable."

"Whatever that means," Dad said with a sigh.

Then, seeing Laurel's anxious, puzzled face, her father went on to explain what it did mean. Dr. Fullbright had shared the report from the Mental Health Clinic quite fully. James was going to need special help in learning.

He should be in a classroom with other boys and girls with intellectual handicaps, taught by a teacher specially trained to help such children learn. He should be able to learn to read in spite of his slow beginning. Laurel had not been a poor teacher. It was just that James had not been ready to read at six. If he had the help he needed, he should be able someday to earn his own living. He would never be a lawyer or an engineer or a minister, but he might work well in a factory or as a gas station attendant.

"Dick says that James should not have to sit in a regular class in school and fail day after day. A specially trained teacher would be able to give him tasks which he could do successfully and which would help him to learn," Dad explained. There was a weariness in his voice as he said this which Laurel did not understand.

Her heart was bright with hope. She had known for a long time that school was bad for James. He was growing more and more certain that he was "no good." More and more often he came home listless and dull or angry at everyone. Now all that would be changed. Now . . .

"There's one problem," Dad said bitterly, not meeting her shining eyes.

Mama and Aunt Jessica waited with her to hear what it was.

"Here in Riverside, we have Special Education all right," he told them. They still waited. "But they don't take any child into the special classes until he is nine years old."

"But James is only seven . . ." Laurel breathed. Looking around at the three adults, she appealed to them. "That would mean he'd have to fail twice more before he got help. That can't be right."

"That is right. Well, no, it is wrong — but that is how it is. Some cities start them at eight. Dick Fullbright says that there are hardly any classes for children under eight. All we can do is wait."

That night, Laurel dreamed she and James were running away. Almost at once, the dream grew muddled. They were monarch butterflies. "We have to go back," James shouted at her. "You're going to fail," Laurel told him. "You're going to fail." James turned with a sweep of his orange and black wings. He did not seem to hear her. "We have to go back," he repeated. And then, suddenly, she was alone, standing on her own two feet, in a strange valley. "I must be in California," she thought and wakened.

The day before school began, Elspeth slipped out of the house and was missing for over an hour. Right after supper, she and her mother left. At the last minute, Laurel could not find anything to say. She waved frantically but she could not see the departing car for tears.

That night James moved upstairs into the room that had been Lindsay's. That night, he wet his bed for the first time since the holidays began.

21

Bravely Home

The Rosses were at breakfast. Dad was reading the *Globe*. Mama was telling Lindsay to stop making islands in her porridge.

Laurel looked around at her family. Everything that was happening seemed like an echo of a morning that was past, a morning before Mama's accident, before Puff, before Aunt Jessica and Elspeth coming. It was as though time had slipped, somehow, and shed six or seven weeks. More and more, as Laurel went forward, the difficult and exciting days she had just lived through were taking on the quality of a dream.

James had wakened her in the night when he wet the bed. She had not had to get up with him for a long time. Although she followed him to a new bedroom, the routine of getting him and his sheets changed had been completely familiar. She even caught herself giving him a hand with his clean pajamas although after Aunt Jessica's schooling, he needed no assistance.

When she had opened her eyes this morning, she had seen the bed which Elspeth had used, still standing in its place. Without sheets or a pillow, without the yellow quilt Elspeth had so loved, the bed was no longer Elspeth's — and today, sometime, Dad was going to move it back down to the garage. Then there would be nothing to prove that Laurel Ross had ever shared her bedroom with another girl.

"Lindsay Ross, *eat!* Mrs. Birch will be here to take you to nursery school in twenty minutes. She's promised to cope, John, till I'm on my feet again," Mama said.

Mrs. Birch! To Laurel, Mrs. Birch now seemed to belong in another life, a life she had imagined was finished. She had a new life now. Her days were full of being Marguerite, talking with Elspeth, mothering Lindsay, watching over James from afar, caring for Puff, wondering about Alice, wondering about Barbara . . .

"James, you're poking too," Mama said.

She sounded tired already. It must be hard for her to sit there helpless, watching them mismanage things. She went on, her voice strained, "Laurel won't wait for you all day, you know."

"But, Susan . . ." Dad started. He stopped, looked at his wife's tense face, thought better of whatever he had planned to say and turned to the second section of the paper.

Laurel looked at James. He was bending over his plate, shoving food into his mouth. He did not say a word.

I'm so glad Mama's home, Laurel told herself forlornly. Everything will be much better now that she's home.

She tried to think of other things, bolstering things, things that would make the day bearable.

But the play was over. She would not be Marguerite again.

"I thought my bed was full of bees, Mama," Lindsay remembered. "I could hear them buzzing right behind me all the way down the stairs."

Mama reached out and ruffled the white-gold curls. Her face softened.

"You're a silly goose," she said fondly. "It was only a dream."

Laurel sat very still and did not look at anyone.

I didn't even hear her go, she thought.

If only Elspeth were there, if only she could glance up and meet Elspeth's eyes, sharing each new hurt, lightening the surprising heaviness of her heart. . . .

Perhaps it was Lindsay's dream of bees that reminded her, but all of a sudden Laurel remembered the dream she herself had had in which she and James had been monarch butterflies. She tried to recapture the details of the dream but they melted away as she reached in her mind for them.

"More toast, Laurel?" Mama said, studying her daughter's absorbed face.

"No . . . no, thanks," Laurel said absently, not moving.

Once, she had dreamed of escaping, of flying away into a free and sunlit world. Suddenly it came to her that in the last few weeks she had actually done it. She had flown away as surely as the monarchs did. She had escaped being that other girl whose only friend was her younger brother. She had become another Laurel, perhaps the Laurel she was meant to be. She glossed over the difficult and hurtful days and remembered how full, how interesting, how different life had been during that space of time.

But now, like the butterflies, she had had to turn and come back. Without her ever guessing it, the old world had been waiting for her all the while. This very minute, she was Mama's daughter again, James's big sister. And there was Mrs. Birch at the back door!

Laurel pushed her chair back with a clatter.

But, when she spoke, the words came dully.

"Come on, James," she said.

Then James spoke up.

"I can go by myself." His voice was defiant, shrill, a little frightened. "I'm not a baby. I don't need *her!*"

He jerked his head to indicate Laurel but his eyes were on Mama. Mama stared at him.

"James!" she cried. Dad put down his paper and cleared his throat uncomfortably. Laurel stood still, waiting to see if this, too, were a dream.

"I go by myself every day now," James was sounding surer of himself. His chin stuck out stubbornly. "Aunt Jessica taught me the way. I don't need Laurel. I'm too big to walk with her."

"Can he really?" Mama appealed to her husband and her older daughter.

Laurel opened her mouth to tell how she and Elspeth

had followed James every day for the last two weeks of school, but she closed it before the words came out. She discovered, all at once, that she did not want James to know. He had been brave, really brave. The little boy who so often boasted about courage he did not possess should not be robbed of the true courage he had shown when he thought he was entirely alone.

"He can do it, Mama. He's been doing it for days. He'll be all right," Laurel backed him up.

Dad added further assurance.

A few minutes later, Laurel was out on the street, walking to school by herself.

Maybe those weeks, which seemed so unreal and dreamlike now, had made some difference after all. James had come to her for help in the night, but he had swung off down the sidewalk jauntily this morning, five minutes ahead of her, his lips puckered up in what he called a whistle.

All morning, Laurel Ross was in the middle of a crowd of boys and girls her own age. All morning, Laurel sat and worked and thought alone. Barbara West raised her head more than once to look back down the row to where Laurel sat. Laurel did not know that Barbara watched her. She was lost in a private world which was neither the old world she remembered, the world before Elspeth, nor the new world which had been hers and Elspeth's together. She was searching, trying to find where she belonged, whither she was bound, perhaps even who she was. But, on this first day, everything seemed strange, herself most of all.

"Hi, Marguerite old thing," Herb Schmidt grinned as

he passed her desk on his way to the pencil sharpener. That was something new, the sparkling look of fun remembered which gleamed at her from Herb's bright eyes.

Laurel grinned back.

"Good morning, Nicholas, my lad," she returned with mock pomposity.

Would the Laurel of six weeks ago have said that?

Home again, she sat at the table at noon and studied the top of James's head, bent over his soup. There was no special class for James yet, but it had been worth it all the same, facing up to Dad and making him understand how badly James needed help. Her father was not the only one who had learned to understand James better since that night. Aunt Jessica, direct and harsh as she had seemed at times, had opened all their eyes to James's capabilities.

After lunch, when Mama reminded, "Help James with his coat, dear," Laurel looked at her mother with surprise.

"He doesn't need any help," she said flatly. "He puts on his own things."

When James did exactly that and ran out of the house without a backward glance, Laurel suddenly saw, in her mind's eye, the little boy Mama had left when she went to the hospital. She remembered how desperately he had clung to her that day when she had found him in the snow. He was still failing of course. His only passing grade on his Christmas report card had been in arithmetic computation, and it would be at least a year before he would begin to get the kind of help he needed. Still, he was coming along, was James. He was growing up.

"He isn't a baby any longer," Mama said wistfully.

Until that instant, Laurel had thought she was the only one who missed that other, younger James. She bent and gave Mama an impulsive hug, the kind of spur-of-the-moment hug which Mama herself gave so often and which her children had wanted so badly sometimes while Aunt Jessica had been running the house.

Then she straightened, blushed faintly and hurried off to school too.

She was on her way home again when the scattered pieces started to come together. She was thinking of Elspeth. It seemed to her that all day long she had been thinking of and missing Elspeth.

Why, I'm lonely, she thought, with a queer jolt of surprise.

She was lonely because she had made a real friend. That other Laurel, the Laurel she had been so short a time before, had never had someone her own age to share things with, someone who made every joke twice as funny because she was there to laugh with you, and someone who felt your disappointments as keenly as though they were her own.

I wanted a friend but I didn't really know, back then, what it would mean to have one, she worked it out slowly. If Elspeth had never come, I wouldn't be lonely . . . not lonely like this.

"Laurel, hurry!" Barbara West shouted, running toward her. "It's James!"

Laurel guessed at once what was wrong. That crowd of boys who had set on James before! She ran as hard as she

could after Barbara. When they reached the corner, they were side by side.

"Wait," Barbara gasped, putting out an arm and holding Laurel back.

"But James . . ." Laurel panted, trying to push past her.

"Look," Barbara said simply.

Herb Schmidt was at James's side. Kevin Wells, from the third grade, was standing next to him too. Two blond boys, whose names Laurel did not know, but who were clearly brothers, were busy making snowballs for Herb, who was giving directions. Sam Goldberry was hopping off his bike and coming to join in.

"All right, James, let 'em have it!" Herb yelled.

Snowballs were flying thick and fast now but James was in no danger. Laurel heard his high, little boy's laugh ringing out.

"I'm brave!" he screamed joyfully. "Watch out, you guys, I'm brave!"

"But . . . but . . . I thought . . ." Laurel stammered, bewildered.

"James was just a block ahead of me," Barbara explained hurriedly. "A gang of them blocked the sidewalk and started calling him names. I knew you weren't far behind so I ran back, but I saw Herb first, so I called to him, 'Help Laurel's brother!' and I pointed."

"Hey, let's build a fort and then we can really play," a dark boy, a head taller than James, called out.

"A couple of you come on our side so it'll be fair," Herb acted on the suggestion.

Jack Rogers and George Gutzmann came. From where Laurel stood, she could see the sheepish look they gave James. The swagger of the one boy and the shamble of the other showed their embarrassment. But Herb was a hero with all the boys — and Herb seemed to have forgotten that this bunch had been tormenting a seven-year-old.

"Let's see you make a proper snowball, James," he said.

James tried but the snow, although it was good for packing, mushed between his mittens. Herb stooped for a fresh handful and started giving lessons.

Laurel blazed with anger for an instant, as she saw the other boys gathering around — James's friends and his enemies together. Then she remembered Elspeth prophesying that James might find friends of his own, given a chance. And she saw, though still dimly, how clever Herb was being, making two opposing gangs into one friendly group. She did not put what she felt into words but she did know, with sudden, warm relief that she would not have to follow James again. James would really and truly be all right on his own.

"We'd better go before James spots us," Barbara said.

They had walked a block together before Laurel realized that the wall separating Barbara and herself had tumbled down. She looked at the other girl with such a baffled expression in her brown eyes that Barbara laughed.

"Elspeth came to see me yesterday," she confessed. They walked on slowly as she explained. "She told me about James . . . Where we used to live, there were some girls in my class . . . well, I thought they were my friends, until one day they started hiding from me and whispering things to each other when I was there. I didn't know what had happened until one of them told me that her mother didn't want her to go around with a girl who had a crazy sister."

Laurel was appalled. She searched for something to say but no words came. Barbara struggled on, her voice low, her face red.

"Well, Alice isn't crazy. Even if she were, she's my sister. I get mad at her. She does such dumb things sometimes and people stare and I hate it. But I love her too and I know she doesn't mean to make me feel . . . oh, I don't know. Anyway, I thought you'd found out about her when you didn't wait for me that day — and then, you said something about if I had a sister or brother who was 'different.' I know now that you didn't mean Alice, but I thought it was all happening over again. I guess I'm the 'crazy' one," she finished unhappily.

Laurel, without knowing she was going to, snickered suddenly. Barbara's flush darkened and she started to turn away, but Laurel caught her arm.

"I was just thinking that we must have looked pretty nutty ourselves that morning when you saw us shadowing James — the way we dodged behind trees and peered around houses and everything!"

Barbara grinned crookedly.

"You did look a bit queer," she agreed in a voice that shook.

Laurel sobered abruptly.

"Barb, I'm awfully sorry Goldilocks died," she offered.

Barbara accepted that with a nod.

"Yes . . . well, she was getting old. Hamsters only live to be around two." Then she took a deep breath and threw at Laurel, "I asked Miss Roe if I could have Elspeth's desk and she said 'Yes.' "

"Good," Laurel said.

She wanted to say much more. She wanted to tell Barbara that she understood about Alice. She knew all about the burden of aloneness Barbara had carried; she had carried it herself for so long. Something in Laurel reached out after Elspeth, loving her, thanking her for all that she, Laurel, had learned about being a friend and having a friend.

Friendship was "a fragile thing" as Aunt Jessica's friend had written. But it did shine like a butterfly's wing. Everything around Laurel — Salters' tiny evergreens capped with snow, the pearly gray sky, the curly russet dog galloping around the corner, even the blue car parked next to the nearby curb, all ordinary, everyday things — shone, took on a touch of magic. This was how friendship began, Laurel knew. It was like the moment when you first believed, inside yourself, that Christmas was coming. Christmas itself was lovely but it did not have the tiptoe excitement, the stirring of wonder and praise which were yours in that other moment when you looked ahead and saw Christmas waiting.

Or spring coming. It happened then too. The sun felt almost hot, all at once. The wind had a fresh damp smell. Snow still covered the ground but you knew, with a lifting of your heart, that the thaw was near. Spring was just around the corner.

Laurel's inner vision shifted suddenly and deepened. She remembered the monarchs whom she had thought so like herself — escaping only to have to turn and come again to the world they had left. Now she saw that she had missed the truth. When the monarchs returned, after their long journey, they did not find the old world waiting any more than she had. They left a land shrouded in autumn. They came back to a world quickening with spring, bright with fresh beginnings.

She wished she could explain all of this to Barbara. But few of her tumbling thoughts were in neat sentences. Nothing she could say would make sense. Barbara had probably never heard of the migration of monarch butterflies.

Laurel turned to the girl at her side and said, "Come on over to my house and see if Puff's awake."

"He won't be," Barbara stated sensibly.

"I know it, but come on over anyway," Laurel said.

She looked right at Barbara then and all the excitement and wonder in her heart was there, shining back at her, in Barbara's smile.

"Okay," Barbara said simply.

And they walked on together, not needing words.